HIDDEN WOODS
Echoes of the Lost Twin

AANYA DIANE

HIDDEN WOODS

Echoes of the Lost Twin

AANYA DIANE

BLUEROSE PUBLISHERS
India | U.K.

Copyright © Aanya Diane 2024

All rights reserved by author. No part of this publication may be reproduced, stored in a retrieval system or transmitted in any form or by any means, electronic, mechanical, photocopying, recording or otherwise, without the prior permission of the author. Although every precaution has been taken to verify the accuracy of the information contained herein, the publisher assumes no responsibility for any errors or omissions. No liability is assumed for damages that may result from the use of information contained within.

BlueRose Publishers takes no responsibility for any damages, losses, or liabilities that may arise from the use or misuse of the information, products, or services provided in this publication.

For permissions requests or inquiries regarding this publication, please contact:

BLUEROSE PUBLISHERS
www.BlueRoseONE.com
info@bluerosepublishers.com
+91 8882 898 898
+4407342408967

ISBN: 978-93-6783-858-7

Cover design: Shivam
Typesetting: Namrata Saini

First Edition: November 2024

CONTENTS

CHAPTER ONE
The Fateful Forest   1

CHAPTER TWO
A Glimmer of Hope   4

CHAPTER THREE
Unravelling Mysteries   12

CHAPTER FOUR
Embracing the Truth   22

CHAPTER FIVE
The Coven's Reunion   44

CHAPTER SIX
Igniting the Spirit   54

CHAPTER SEVEN
Through the Lenses of Time   63

CHAPTER EIGHT
The Hidden Reality ... 83

CHAPTER NINE
Veiled in Memory ... 101

CHAPTER TEN
Beneath the Moonlight ... 123

CHAPTER ELEVEN
The Path Ahead ... 155

CHAPTER TWELVE
Light at Last ... 201

CHAPTER THIRTEEN
The Curtain Falls ... 212

CHAPTER ONE

The Fateful Forest

Deep within the depths of Enchanted Summit, where the air was thick with the scent of damp earth and ancient magic, a sinister stillness had settled, for it was whispered that the people who lived there had met a dark fate.

Not far away, the city of Midnight Woods was rumoured to have some strange animals which defied the laws of nature.

The people of Glendon, which was near the Enchanted Summit and Midnight Woods, knew how to avoid these two places, but there was no promise of evading these zones, given that dreadful happenings occur from time to time.

The people thought that the city of Midnight Woods had some peculiar animals which kill people. But Aria knew that it wasn't an animal.

Aria was an orphaned quiet, withdrawn eleven-year-old who kept her thoughts and emotions bottled up, rarely speaking unless necessary. She had no friends at school and preferred to stay in the background, keeping everyone at a distance.

Aunt Jesse Miller and Uncle Harold Miller, who had raised her after the tragic loss of her parents, had always told her they had died in a car crash. But the truth of that night had always felt incomplete, like a puzzle with missing pieces.

Aria and Jayden, her twin, had shared an extraordinary sibling bond. Whether they had been playing games, exploring their surroundings, or simply enjoying each other's company, their deep connection had been evident in everything they did.

Until one tragic night, about a month ago, as Aria and Jayden had wandered through the forest, Aria had tied a thread with one half of a heart pendant onto Jayden's wrist. Just as he had been about to do the same for her, he had accidentally dropped his half.

When Aria had bent down to pick it up, Jayden had suddenly been dragged away into Midnight Woods. All Aria had heard was Jayden screaming.

Desperate, she had tried calling his name, but no sound had come from her mouth. Her body had gone limp, as if struck by a stone.

Opening her palm, she had seen the half-heart pendant still clutched in her hand. A tear had fallen onto the pendant, making it glisten. Still crying, Aria had struggled to make her way home.

In the quiet of the night, Aria stirred from her nightmare, her cheeks stained with tears and sweat glistening on her forehead.

Even after a month had passed, she still struggled to accept what had happened.

Her brother was gone indeed.

CHAPTER TWO

A Glimmer of Hope

The alarm clock buzzed, signalling the start of another day. Aria began her familiar routine of getting ready. After a quick shower and a simple breakfast, her aunt, Jesse, stood by the table, arms crossed.

'Sit down and eat,' she ordered, her voice firm.

'I'm not hungry, Mrs. Miller,' Aria muttered.

Aunt Jesse narrowed her eyes and shoved the plate closer. 'I didn't ask if you were hungry. You'll eat it.'

Aria hesitated, feeling the weight of her aunt's stern gaze. 'Thanks,' she mumbled as she reluctantly sat down, knowing there was no point in arguing.

She quickly gobbled a piece of bread and quenched it with water. Aria gathered her books and slung her bag over her shoulder. The walk to school was a silent one, the weight of unspoken thoughts hanging heavy in the air.

As the school gates loomed ahead, she braced herself for another day of misery, wondering if anything would ever change. The towering iron bars, now rusted and cold, felt suffocating, trapping her in a routine that had lost all meaning.

Three years ago, these very gates held a different kind of memory—one that brought warmth, comfort, and the sound of her parents' laughter as they dropped her and Jayden off every morning.

She could almost hear her father's voice, telling them to have a good day, and her mother's gentle reminder not to forget their lunchboxes. The sight of Jayden waving excitedly as they ran ahead, carefree and full of life, made the emptiness now feel even more overwhelming.

Aria felt a lump form in her throat, her chest tightening with grief. The ache of missing her parents had never dulled, and in moments like this, it was as sharp as ever.

'Why did everything have to change?' she whispered to herself, her gaze fixed on the gate as if it held all the answers. She felt so far away from the girl who used to run through these gates with Jayden, with nothing but school worries on her mind.

Now, those were the days she longed for—before the world turned upside down.

Aria swallowed the tears that threatened to fall, trying to push the memories aside as she trudged through the gates alone, feeling the absence of her parents like a shadow that followed her everywhere.

Everything had changed since they'd been gone, and every day that passed, she wondered how much more she could endure before the weight of their absence crushed her completely.

'Alright, class,' barked Professor Loomy, who was Aria's science teacher, 'Turn to page two hundred ninety-four. Here, you'll find the diagram of an Amoeba, which is a protozoan. And on page two hundred ninety-eight,' she droned on, 'You'll see a sketch of a Paramecium. Now, Paramecium is also a protozoan and is unicellular.'

And so, the lecture continued.

Finally, when school ended—which felt like the longest, most pointless day ever—Aria walked out of the gates and did the one thing she actually liked: chatting with Grandma Elleira who ran the shop near the school.

Grandma Elleira was one of the most cheerful people in Glendon. She wore round spectacles perched on her crooked nose and had a unique charm about her. At times, she acted more like a teenager than an old lady.

'Hi, Grandma,' Aria greeted warmly. 'How's your day going?' Though Aria and Grandma Elleira weren't related by blood, she was fond of calling her 'Grandma.'

'Not so well, sweetie,' Elleira replied with a sigh. 'My knitting business isn't going as well as I'd hoped. People say it's outdated and a waste of time.'

'I'm sorry to hear that,' Aria said sympathetically. 'But I think it's wonderful. It gives people a nostalgic feeling.'

'Thank you, my dear,' Grandma Elleira said with a soft smile. 'Now, have you discovered anything new about the legends?'

'Yeah, I found a couple of references at the library.' Aria placed two books on the table. The titles read *Vampires and Witches – Are the Legends True?* and *How Are Supernatural Creatures Different from Humans Like Us?*

Elleira raised an eyebrow, giving her a sceptical look. 'You've moved on from dwarfs and werewolves to vampires and witches?'

'Well, I was reading about werewolves when I stumbled across this. I thought I'd explore it. And as I read more, they seemed... more relatable. Besides,' Aria's voice faltered, 'I'm desperate to understand what really took my brother away.'

'Alright, I've heard people talk about witches often,' said Elleira, still uncertain. 'You know, they're rumoured to be in the Enchanted Summit near Glendon.'

'Wait,' Aria said, her voice full of disbelief. 'You're telling me witches are real?'

'I think they are, my dear,' Elleira replied. 'Why else do you think people talk about them so often? Besides, it's worth looking into.'

'If you believed witches were real, why didn't you tell me sooner? We could've saved so much time researching those ridiculous legends about dwarfs and werewolves.'

'At first, it all seemed like nonsense,' Elleira admitted, 'But the more I read, the more I felt witches might be the key—much more than those dwarfs and werewolves.'

'You've been reading?' Aria asked, mildly surprised.

'It's never too late to read,' Elleira shrugged. 'I can lend you some of the books if you're interested.'

'Sure.' Aria replied.

Grandma Elleira searched in her tiny shack and placed some battered, old-fashioned books on the table.

'Thanks, Grandma,' said Aria.

'Anytime, dear,' said Elleira. 'Though, I think you'll have to go; it's nearly dusk.'

'Oh, right,' said Aria, glancing up. It was dusk already. Time always seemed to fly when she talked with this old lady. Despite her age, their conversations made minutes feel like seconds. 'I should get going. I'll read the book and let you know tomorrow. Bye, Grandma.'

'Bye, my dear,' said Elleira.

Aria raced back home as she always did. This was no different from her morning walk to school, except for the orange sky instead of the usual blue. Earlier, these morning walks used to be one of the best times, playing with her brother. Now, they felt empty and meaningless.

She reached home, feeling as though it had taken a million hours, and went straight to her room. She shut the door with a heavy thud, shutting out the noise of the outside world. With a sigh, Aria collapsed onto her bed, utterly exhausted.

But she wasn't ready to sleep. Not yet.

Instead, Aria reached for the book Elleira had given her, its edges tattered and its spine barely holding together. The title, Maria's Diary, was etched in faded gold, barely legible through the wear of time. As she began flipping through the brittle pages, her pulse quickened. Maybe, just maybe, there was something in these pages that could help her make sense of it all. On the seventh page, she saw a list of wizard names.

Found in an old diary by Maria in the 1800's, wizards and cloaks, rather reveal themselves to the open world. Reading the diary, researchers found out that Maria wasn't quite sure what kind of intentions they had—good or bad. Her diary had a long list of names. Back then, these wizards and witches were renowned for their enchanting skill of magic.

1. Arthur
2. Persephone
3. Alice
4. Phineas
5. Arielle
6. Reginald
7. Gabrielle

All of these names were old fashioned and vintage, yet there was some kind of magic in their names—as though they hinted at something mystical. What if these wizards and witches still walked among us? Aria pondered silently.

What if it was one of them who snatched her brother away? Yet, even if they had, the true question remained: Why?

What was a witch or a wizard going to do with an ordinary human when they had extraordinary powers?

Aria had no clue.

CHAPTER THREE

Unravelling Mysteries

The cereal was soggy, the milk was warm, and the day was usual. Another day in the prison of school awaited, and Aria couldn't muster a shred of enthusiasm.

She trudged through the hallways, dodging clusters of giggles and laughter. One of Aria's classmates caught up to her, whose face was lit with a smile, 'Hey, did you finish the history homework?'

'No,' grumbled Aria, 'Didn't see the point. It's not like Professor Johnson reads them.'

Professor Johnson, a man likely in his mid-50s, had been teaching History for as long as anyone could remember. He assigned homework to his students on time but seemed too lazy to actually grade it.

She sighed, used to Aria's perpetual grumpiness. 'Well, I guess that's true. Anyways, see you in class.' she said, right after the bell of the first period rang.

To no one's surprise, Professor Johnson did not ask for the homework, and he continued with his lecture on *European colonisation*.

As the day dragged on, Aria found herself in the crowded cafeteria, poking at the unappetizing lump on her tray. Just then, a football flew across the room, narrowly missing her head. Aria glared at the table of jocks who were laughing obnoxiously. They ignored her, of course, returning to their loud, pointless conversation.

Sighing, Aria pushed her tray aside, losing her appetite completely. Aria had a test at the last period, but her brain felt too foggy to focus on anything academic.

The bell rang. She made her way through the sea of students, dodging backpacks and elbows. Professor Smith was droning about algebraic expressions like it was the most fascinating thing in the world.

'How can anyone find this stuff interesting?' Aria muttered, 'I mean, seriously, who cares about x and y and all that nonsense? I bet even Professor Smith doesn't use them outside the classroom. She probably goes home and reads novels or something, not solve for x and y.'

Aria could feel her eyes glazing over as she stared at the whiteboard, trying to make sense of the squiggles that Professor Smith wrote. Her notebook was open in front of her, but she hadn't written a single word.

Aria really tried to focus. She picked up her pencil and pretended to take notes, but her mind kept wandering somewhere else, in the world of witches.

She imagined a blonde witch who had a staff with a green gem on top of it. Aria had read last night that these wizards and witches had a staff (not a wand), with a green gem on top of it. Maria's diary was huge (she must have lived a long old life, bless her, for there were so many pages) and was apparently helpful in her quest.

She believed in them, but were they actually real?

Right after school ended, Aria went to Elleira's shop, where the old lady waited, whose face was lit with an evident smile.

'Hello, my dear' greeted Grandma Elleira, 'How are you doing today?'

'So far, the usual,' said Aria, 'How's it for you?'

'Same old, same old,' Grandma Elleira replied. 'One of the customers barked at me today for selling a bumblebee knitted piece instead of a flower one. Well, what can you do?' she added with a sigh. 'I may be an old lady, but that doesn't give anyone the right to shout at me just because of my eyesight. But enough about that,' she said, wrapping up the story. 'I'm here to talk to you, and only you.'

'Thanks, Grandma,' said Aria, 'I spent last night reading the book you gave me, and you were right—it made everything seem so much more believable. Especially the part about wizards rumoured to be living right near Glendon.'

'Alright, and what did you find? Anything peculiar?' Elleira asked with interest.

'Well, not much,' said Aria. 'Mostly just a list of wizards and witches' names. I also learned that back then, wizards didn't wear cloaks—they carried staffs with green gems on top.'

'Well, you've covered almost everything.' Elleira remarked.

Aria's eyes sparkled with curiosity. 'Do you think it's true? That there are wizards living so close to us?'

Grandma Elleira paused, thinking carefully. 'It's very possible. People with magic often live quietly, blending in to avoid attention. Glendon has a long history of magic, so it wouldn't surprise me if wizards lived nearby.'

'I see,' Aria said thoughtfully.

'Did you read the passage on page five hundred sixty-one?' Elleira asked suddenly.

'Erm, no. What's so special about it?' Aria asked as she opened her bag and rummaged for the book.

'Well,' said Grandma Elleira, 'It's not much, but it might be everything you need to know.'

Aria flipped through the pages until she found the page. The book was large and worn, making it difficult to flick through.

'Here it is,' Grandma Elleira pointed to a small passage on the page.

Some wizards and witches showed exceptional interest in anadromes. They were known to use these in ancient incantations or to conceal their identities from the human world.

'What are anadromes?' Aria asked, intrigued.

'They're words or names that read differently when spelled backward. For example, 'desserts' backward is 'stressed'.' Elleira explained.

'Oh, that's interesting. But why are you showing this to me? Is it really important?' Aria asked.

'Absolutely. We need to understand what defences they might have in place, so we can uncover their true identities.' Grandma Elleira said seriously.

'Alright, Grandma. I'll look into this more today and let you know tomorrow.' Aria promised.

'I know you can do it, sweetie. You're clever.' Elleira encouraged.

'Thanks, Grandma.' said Aria.

'And before you go, dear,' Grandma Elleira said suddenly, 'Would you mind coming inside? I want to show you my latest pieces.'

Aria didn't really feel like stepping into the old shop, but she couldn't say no to Elleira. She nodded and followed her inside.

The room was dimly lit by a vintage lamp and filled with knitted pieces that Aria couldn't help but admire. How could anyone not want to buy these? There was something almost magical about them.

But as Aria moved past the colourful knitted pieces, something else caught her eye. Among the cheerful creations was an object that seemed out of place. It was a long, stick-like object, half-hidden among the items.

Curious, Aria moved closer. The object was rough to the touch and looked incredibly old.

She adjusted her position, letting the light from the window illuminate the object. As she leaned in, squinting to see the details, she noticed faint carvings etched into the wood.

'Grandma, what's this?' Aria asked, pointing to the stick.

'Oh, that,' Grandma Elleira said, her voice suddenly tense. 'It's my walking stick, dear.'

'But you walk without a stick.' Aria pointed out.

'Well,' Elleira began, clearly trying to change the subject, 'I used to use it because of severe knee pain. But a kind customer, who was a doctor, offered to do surgery, and I don't need it anymore.'

'Oh, I see. I'm sorry.' said Aria.

'Don't be, dear,' said Elleira kindly. 'Feel free to ask me anything. Let me know what you find out tomorrow.' she added, glancing at the old-fashioned clock.

'I guess that's my cue to leave,' said Aria with a smile. 'See you tomorrow, Grandma.'

'Take care, my dear.' Elleira said cheerfully.

Aria stumbled back home. The whole walk felt like a dream, and by the time she stepped through the front door, she couldn't even remember how she got there.

She just kind of floated to the dinner table, picked her food, her mind elsewhere.

She was exhausted, every bone in her body screamed for sleep, but there was no way she was ready to crash just yet.

With a heavy sigh, she grabbed a piece of paper and a pen, plopping down at her desk. She copied down names of wizards and witches from Maria's diary.

'Okay, let's see...Arthur, Persephone, Alice...' she mumbled, her pen scratching against the paper. She began reversing the letters in each name, seeing if they formed anything interesting. Most of them ended up as gibberish. 'Phineas is Saeniph. That's just dumb,'

Her eyes narrowed as she crossed out the nonsensical ones. The list was shrinking rapidly, but then, something caught her eye. She stared at the reversed letters of one name for a solid minute, her heart pounding faster and faster. 'No way,' she whispered, her hand trembling. Aria didn't even bother to copy other names.

It was so shocking, so unbelievable, that she nearly fell out of her chair. Her tiredness vanished in an instant, replaced by a surge of adrenaline. The name she had uncovered changed everything.

Arthur - ~~Ruthra~~

Persephone - ~~Enohpesrep~~

Alice - ~~Ecila~~

Phineas - ~~Saeniph~~

Arielle - Elleira

She stared at the paper, her mouth hanging open. 'No way,' she whispered, gripping the edges of her desk. 'This can't be real.'

Suddenly, everything clicked into place.

'There's only one reason why Grandma got so tense whenever I mentioned the stick,' Aria murmured, her eyes wide with realisation. 'It must have been the staff. A witch's staff with a gem on top.' She could almost see it now, glowing with an eerie light.

The reason Grandma Elleira became so uneasy whenever we talked about wizards and witches... there's only one explanation... The truth heavily settled upon her shoulders. The more she said, the more it made sense to her.

'Grandma Elleira is a witch,' she whispered, the words feeling both foreign and undeniable. The ordinary world she knew had just been turned upside down, and she had to find out more.

She had to talk to Elleira, no matter what secrets were about to be revealed.

CHAPTER FOUR

Embracing the Truth

Taking a deep breath, she turned towards the shop where Grandma sat knitting, seemingly oblivious to the storm brewing in Aria's mind. 'I have to know the truth,' Aria said to herself, steeling her nerves for the conversation that was about to change everything.

With determination, Aria walked towards the shop, Maria's Diary clutched tightly in her hand.

'Grandma,' Aria began, her voice steady but her heart racing, 'Can we talk for a minute?'

Grandma Elleira looked up, her eyes twinkling with warmth. 'Hello, dear. I didn't expect to see you this early. Of course, we can talk. What's on your mind?'

'You gave me the clue of anadromes, right?'

'Yes,' said Grandma simply.

Aria hesitated for a moment, then took a deep breath. 'I've been thinking about some things... especially about the name Arielle and how it reverses to Elleira.'

A flicker of recognition crossed Grandma Elleira's face, her hands pausing mid-knit. 'Oh,' she said softly, her voice suddenly more serious. 'I see you've been quite the detective, haven't you?'

'Grandma, please,' Aria pressed, her eyes searching Elleira's face. 'I need to know the truth. Why do you get so tense when we talk about wizards and witches?'

Grandma Elleira sighed deeply, setting her knitting aside. She motioned for Aria to sit down beside her. 'It's time you knew,' she said, her voice heavy with a mixture of relief and sadness. 'That stick you saw yesterday in my shack. It was a witch's staff. My staff.'

'Wait, you knew I saw the stick?' Aria asked, her voice tinged with surprise and confusion.

Grandma Elleira nodded calmly. 'Yes, I did. In fact, I showed you that area deliberately, so you would find the stick.'

Aria's eyes widened. 'Wait. Hang on,' she said, as the fog in her mind began to clear, 'You wanted me to know...'

Grandma Elleira met her gaze, a serious yet gentle look in her eyes. 'I wanted you to know that I am a witch.'

Silence settled between them, thick and hefty. The distant chatter of people seemed to magnify, as though someone had turned up the volume on a speaker, filling the quiet area with a background hum.

'In movies, they call this a plot twist.' said Aria finally, attempting to lighten the mood, though her voice trembled slightly.

Grandma Elleira chuckled softly, the tension easing a bit. 'Life can be full of plot twists, my dear. And *sometimes*, they lead us to the truth we've been searching for.'

'So, it's true. You're a witch.' remarked Aria again stupidly.

Grandma Elleira nodded slowly. 'Yes, I am. I've kept it a secret all these years to protect everyone. The world isn't always kind to those who are different.'

Aria's mind buzzed with questions. 'But why hide it? And why was the staff hidden away?'

Grandma Elleira's gaze turned distant, her eyes clouding with memories. 'There are dangers, Aria, powerful forces that would seek to use or destroy what they don't understand. When I was young, I wielded my powers openly, thinking I could make the world a better place. But I quickly learned that not everyone shares our values. There were those who wanted to exploit my abilities, to use them for their own dark purposes.'

'Why did you hide the staff?' asked Aria.

Grandma Elleira's eyes glistened with unshed tears. 'After a battle, I realised that my powers, while a gift, also made me a target. I decided to hide my staff and my true identity to protect those I loved. I came here to Glendon, hoping to live a quiet life, free from the dangers of the magical world.'

'But why tell me now?' Aria asked, her voice softening.

Grandma took Aria's hands on her own. 'Because, my dear, you have a right to know. The time has come for you to understand the dangers that come with it. I see the same strength and potential in you that I once had. And with your brother missing, we can't afford to keep secrets any longer.'

Aria took a deep breath, her mind still reeling but her resolve hardening. 'So, what happens now?'

Grandma Elleira's expression softened, her eyes full of pride and anticipation. 'Now, we begin your journey. There's so much you need to learn, and I'll be here to guide you every step of the way.'

Aria nodded, feeling a mixture of fear and excitement bubbling within her. She had a thick strand of hope that her brother could be found after all.

Grandma Elleira smiled warmly, her eyes sparkling with a mix of relief and excitement. 'I knew you would be ready, Aria. There's so much to share, and I've waited a long time for this moment.'

Aria glanced around the shack, which now seemed charged with a new, magical energy. 'Where do we start?' she asked, her curiosity growing by the second.

Grandma Elleira stood up, her movements graceful and purposeful. 'First, we need to find a safe place to talk. Follow me.' She led Aria inside her shop, where she stood firmly opposite a random wall.

'Grandma, why are we standing opposite to a dusty wall?'

'Ahh, it's been a while since I've opened my chamber, dear. It must be here somewhere,' she added, as her eyes flicked around the wall, 'There you are.' she said, as she got her wand.

Grandma Elleira traced a rectangular shape with her wand across the wall. Slowly, but surely, as though it was magical, the rectangular shape she drew was growing into a large door-size like figure.

Grandma Elleira noticed it and so did Aria.

She saw the same wall, but this time with a long, very thin rectangular outline, as though it was a door.

'Wow. This is smart, Grandma. A secret chamber...hidden in plain sight. Is this what was mentioned in Maria's Diary? You know, in the part where wizards and witches liked puzzles?' asked Aria, intrigued.

'Yes, my dear,' said Elleira, as she gave the door a gentle push.

The door gave a loud creak and Aria saw the passage. Inside, there was a short line of steps, and the tunnel was dark.

'Hang on, let me get my torch,' said Elleira as she fumbled a torch in the desks, 'Let's go.'

The tunnel was still dark, even when the torch was on. But Aria didn't mind.

'Whoa,' Aria breathed, following Elleira down the steps, 'I thought that secret rooms only existed in movies.'

The room was filled with shelves of ancient books, jars of strange ingredients, and a large table in the centre with various mystical artifacts scattered across it.

'This was my sanctuary,' Grandma Elleira explained. 'A place where I practised my skills. It's been a long time since I've come to this place.' she added.

Aria wandered around the room, her fingers trailing lightly over the dusty covers of the books. 'What kind of skills did you practise here, Grandma?' she asked, her eyes wide with curiosity.

Elleira smiled, a glimmer of nostalgia in her eyes. 'All sorts of spells, my dear,' said Elleira, 'Though it's been kept secret for generations. This room holds centuries of knowledge and power.'

'Wait, what do you mean by secret?' asked Aria, 'I thought that witches and wizards never conceal themselves?'

'*That* is in the view of Maria.' said Elleira uneasily.

There was something wrong with Grandma's voice. It was as though something had pierced her eyes.

'Grandma, is there something between you and Maria?' asked Aria, determined to know what was exactly going through Elleira's mind.

Grandma looked up, whose eyes were like windows to her soul, wide and unguarded, showing the pain she tried to hide.

'My dear,' said Grandma, 'Sometimes, the person you'd take a bullet for is the one behind the gun.'

'You're talking about trust, more like betrayal.' Aria finally understood.

Grandma nodded.

'Maria was my best friend and the only human who knew about witches and wizards. One day, when my mom had invited Maria over to my house, she saw me practising spells in my room. I generally had a hard time hiding it from my mom—the only way was to keep my mom engaged with other work. Maria saw some streaks of light and heard some noises from my room. Right after I saw her, I immediately hid my staff behind a shelf. Maria was clearly suspicious about me.'

'It was then I took her to my coven—of witches and wizards. They really tried hard to tell her that it was nothing to worry about. But Maria was standing firmly on her ground and not believing anything the others were saying.'

'Finally, we had no other choice but to tell her about our world. Maria was obviously speechless, and it took her some time to get over it. But when she did, she didn't react as badly as I thought she would. The main reason I was hesitant to tell her was because I thought it would ruin our friendship.

'Maria started to get to know more about our world. Every day, we met at the Grand Square in Glendon. Me, my coven and Maria talked about our identities and responsibilities.'

'I just felt that something was off with Maria right after she found out that I was a witch. It was as though she was focused on something. I talked to my coven about

Maria's focus, and they told me it was nothing, just the effect of knowing about our world. But I knew that wasn't true. Finally, in one of our missions with our mortal enemies, Maria's true intentions were revealed.'

Aria could feel the tension mounting, sensing they were on the climax of the suspenseful moment, for Elleira's forehead glistened with sweat, and her speech was punctuated by short, gasping breaths, adding to the suspense of the moment.

'In the midst of chaos of the battle, Maria was nowhere to be seen. She was supposed to be under the coven's protection, as we had asked her to sit out of the battle to keep her safe. While I searched for her amidst fighting my own foe, Maria suddenly appeared, clutching a dagger. I desperately tried to prevent her from throwing it, fearing for her safety, but her eyes were…fierce and cold. With no alternative, I cast a spell to halt the dagger's flight. Before I could question Maria, she was attacked by the opponent I was duelling with.'

'Right after the battle, I discovered that Maria was a traitor. She had carefully orchestrated her actions to attempt to betray me and our coven, acting on behalf of our opponent. Turns out, she already knew about wizards and witches before she saw me casting spells in my room. The vampires had already recruited Maria for gathering information about us so that they could plan their strategies. It was then I realised that the real foe was none other than Maria.'

'The reason the entire coven is now in hiding is because of Maria; her betrayal led to our defeat in battle. We had never experienced defeat before, and now that our enemy has won, it has weakened our powers; they're not as potent as they once were.'

Aria felt overwhelmed by everything Grandma Elleira had told her. Her mind was filled with new information and questions, swirling around like a whirlpool. She had never seen Grandma Elleira talk so much. Aria had judged by the diary that Maria was kind and cheerful.

'I'm sorry, Grandma,' said Aria, filled with emotion, opening her mouth for the first time after Grandma's long talk. Aria looked up and saw Grandma's eyes were brimming with tears waiting to fall, reflecting the sadness she struggled to contain.

'Don't be, my dear,' said Elleira, clearly trying to ease the tension hanging in the air, which was an unfruitful attempt, 'Just remember that betrayal doesn't come from your enemies, it comes from those you trust the most.'

'Right,' Aria nodded, 'But Grandma, can I ask you something?'

'There's plenty you could ask after everything I've told you. But what's the first thing on your mind?'

'Who were their mortal enemies?' asked Aria.

Elleira's gaze darkened. 'Vampires.'

'So, the legends are true,' Aria finally concluded, 'Wizards and witches are in the Enchanted Summit. Wait,' Aria added, 'Does that mean vampires are in Midnight Woods?'

'Yes, they are.' said Grandma Elleira simply.

'But if the entire coven is in Enchanted Summit, then why haven't you joined them? Why are you here in Glendon?'

Grandma sighed. 'After that battle, I was deeply depressed. I felt responsible for our defeat, thinking I had let the entire coven down by trusting Maria, who betrayed us. The coven tried to reassure me, saying that betrayal reveals your true friends. But *that* didn't help me. I took the defeat deep into my heart and have stayed in this town ever since, fearing that my coven would start to blame me.'

'You were afraid of your own friends?' Aria asked incredulously.

Grandma Elleira nodded, her eyes filled with a mixture of sorrow and regret. 'Yes, Aria. Fear and guilt can cloud your judgement, even towards those who care about you the most.'

Aria's heart ached for Grandma Elleira, understanding the weight she had carried all these years. She reached out and took Elleira's hand, squeezing it gently. 'But you're here now, Grandma. And I'm here with you. We can face this together.'

Grandma Elleira smiled weakly, a glimmer of hope lighting up her eyes. 'Thank you, Aria. But we must be cautious. If Maria is still out there, allied with the vampires, finding your brother won't be easy.'

'Grandma, is Maria's past connected to finding my brother?' Aria asked critically.

'It might be, my dear,' Elleira replied. 'According to the diary, Maria is no more. However, there is a slight chance she may still be alive because she was an ally of the vampires.'

'Do you mean that vampires turn all dead humans alive?' Aria inquired.

'Not quite,' said Grandma, 'Generally, when their allies are closely bonded with the vampires and the vampires don't want to lose them, they imprint on their allies by injecting their venom into their palm. When they imprint, they are forever together until witches and wizards stab them twice in their palm. Vampires don't turn *all* dead human beings alive.'

'But why haven't you killed Maria yet?' asked Aria.

Grandma was hesitant. 'For the old times' sake. The best revenge is no revenge. It might bring a moment of satisfaction, but it rarely brings peace, you know.'

Aria frowned, struggling to understand. 'But Maria betrayed us. She caused so much pain. How can you just let her go?'

Grandma sighed deeply. 'It's not about letting her go, Aria. It's about breaking the cycle of hatred and violence. Revenge may seem like the answer, but it only blackens the darkness. We need to focus on finding your brother, not on vengeance.'

Aria nodded slowly, trying to absorb Grandma's wisdom. 'I understand, but it's hard to let go of the anger.'

Grandma placed a gentle hand on Aria's shoulder. 'I know, dear. Anger is a natural response to betrayal. But holding onto it will only poison your heart. We must rise above it, for the sake of our future.'

'Grandma, have you found any trails about vampires?' asked Aria.

'No, my dear. They turn up occasionally, just like with your brother.' said Elleira.

'Hang on,' said Aria, her heart racing, 'Do you mean to say that my brother—my twin, was stolen by a *vampire*?'

Grandma nodded.

Aria's glimmer of hope slowly faded. How could she ever find her brother if he had been taken by a vampire? If even Grandma Elleira seemed uneasy about meeting her old allies, how could Aria possibly face such terrifying creatures on her own? She didn't know the first thing about fighting or defending herself.

Unless...

'Grandma, can I perform spells? You know, to defend myself and all?' asked Aria.

'No, my dear,' replied Grandma. 'Only witches have sole access to their powers. The best we can do for a human is to protect them with our spells, not teach them how to protect themselves.'

Aria's shoulders slumped with disappointment. 'But what if I'm in danger and you're not there to protect me?'

Grandma Elleira placed a reassuring hand on Aria's shoulder. 'That's why we must stick together and stay vigilant. You have other strengths, Aria. Your intelligence, bravery, and determination are just as important as any spell. You will be safe under my watch.'

Aria nodded, though she felt the same feeling just like Maria had been under Grandma's watch.

'So, Grandma, tell me more about magic. Does your coven use wands or staff?'

'Wands or staff, it depends on the situation. If you're in a battle, then you'll need a staff because it has more power than a wand. Wands can be used for general use. You know, like moving one book from here to there. I used to enjoy them a lot. ' Elleira chuckled.

'And what do spells look like?' asked Aria.

'Spells are like rays of light, but it's not like the flashy tricks you see in movies. It's subtle, and it requires a deep understanding of the world around us.'

'I see.' acknowledged Aria.

As Aria continued to explore, she noticed a large, ornate book on the central table, its cover adorned with intricate symbols. 'What's this?' she asked, pointing to the book.

Elleira walked over and gently opened the book, revealing pages filled with hand-drawn diagrams and ancient script. 'This is The Grimoire. It contains spells, potions, and knowledge passed down through generations.'

'Why do you have it? Shouldn't the coven have it?'

'The coven gave me this Grimoire because I was the most responsible user of magic. Others were not,' said Grandma, 'One of my friends, Reginald, blasted his flowerpot by using his staff instead of his wand. It was kind of fun to watch. Though he was later asked to do only potions.' said Grandma, chuckling.

'Who were your other friends, Grandma?' asked Aria, in an attempt to turn the conversation from serious to light.

'All of them were my best friends, Persephone, Gab, Alice, Phineas, Arthur, and there was no denying it. However, at that time, Maria was.' said Grandma, looking down.

Aria's attempt to ease the tension was another fruitless attempt. 'Grandma, can we go and meet your coven, please?'

'I've been thinking about that for quite a while, my dear,' said Grandma, 'The gem of my staff is twinkling in recent days. Usually, it does when a danger is approaching. The staff of other members twinkle only at the last minute. They generally ask me to keep a look at my staff. That's how we would plan and win wars.'

'If there's a need to go, then why can't we go now?' urged Aria.

'Not now, my dear.' said Grandma.

'But the danger is approaching with every passing minute and your coven will be in trouble if they don't know about the danger, you might lose your coven just like you lost Maria, not to mention my brother.' said Aria, fuelling.

'Right. Aria, I understand that you must go, and I accept it. Look, how about I practise some spells? It's been a while since I touched this staff.'

'Grandma, can I be with you?' asked Aria.

'Of course, you can, my dear,' said Grandma, 'Remember, I'm doing this only for you, your brother and my coven.'

'Grandma, did you and your coven save people from the people who were in danger in Glendon?' asked Aria, as she faintly recalled it being mentioned in the diary.

'Yes, we did, my dear,' said Grandma, 'After the battle, I felt that our power was useless. So, I suggested that we could use our power to save the people in need. So, if there was a tiger roaming around the town, trying to kill people, then we would cast a spell to maim the tiger. But, after some time, people thought that we had died because we did not go there. Maria said that wizards and witches did not wear cloaks. Well, she was wrong on that count. The entire coven wore cloaks, and is still wearing them, except me.'

'Why did Maria pour out wrong information in the diary? I thought diaries were supposed to be truthful.'

'Well, do you think Maria would have wanted everyone to know that our world—of witches, wizards and vampires—are real? Of course not. Besides, not *all* information was wrong,' said Grandma, 'she was right about the fact that we used staff, though she did not know that we used wands, so wands were not mentioned in the diary.'

'Wow, there's so much I don't know.' remarked Aria.

'There's so much that *everyone else* doesn't know too.' Grandma corrected.

'Grandma, can we please meet your coven tonight?' asked Aria.

'Tonight? Absolutely not.' said Grandma.

'Why not?' asked Aria.

'Tonight's the third day of the full moon! We can't just stroll around the forest looking for my friends who might be hidden anywhere on a *full moon day*. Look, my dear, I know you want to find your brother no matter what, but your safety is as important as your brother's.' said Grandma.

'What's with the full moon?' asked Aria.

'Aria, vampires come out of hiding on full moon nights. Your brother was taken on one of those nights.' said Elleira.

'Then can we go tomorrow night? It's a gibbous moon, right?' Aria asked, eager to do anything to find her brother.

'Hmm,' said Grandma, her voice thoughtful, as if weighing the risks. After a pause, she added, 'Possibly.'

'Alright, Grandma. I'll come over tomorrow at four, and we can head to the forest.' Aria declared.

'Absolutely, my dear.' Elleira nodded.

'Okay then, I'll see you tomorrow, Grandma.' said Aria, turning to leave, her hand lingering on the door handle.

'Aria, wait,' Grandma Elleira called out suddenly.

Aria froze mid-step, her heart skipping a beat as she turned to face her.

Elleira's eyes, usually filled with warmth, now held a shadow of concern. 'Now that you know about our world...' She hesitated, her voice trailing off as if searching for the right words. 'You'll be vulnerable to all its dangers,' she finally said, her tone heavy with unspoken warnings.

'I'll be careful, Grandma,' Aria replied, her voice firm with determination.

Elleira gave a small, reluctant nod, the lines of worry still etched on her face. Aria offered her a reassuring smile before finally stepping outside, the cool air hitting her as the door closed behind her.

Tomorrow would come, and with it, a journey she could no longer avoid.

CHAPTER FIVE

The Coven's Reunion

As Aria walked away, the weight of the conversation settled in. The revelation about vampires and the full moon added a new layer of urgency to their mission. Aria's thoughts raced as she tried to prepare herself for the challenges ahead. She had always thought of the supernatural as something distant and fictional, but now it was her reality. The stakes were high, and the danger was real.

The next day, Aria spent the morning preparing for the night ahead. She packed a small backpack with essentials—flashlight, water, and some snacks. Her mind buzzed with anticipation and a touch of fear. She knew the journey into the forest would not be easy, but the thought of finding her brother kept her focused and resolute.

By the time the clock struck four, Aria was ready. She made her way to Grandma Elleira's shop, her heart pounding with a mix of anxiety and determination. As she approached the back door, she took a deep breath and knocked.

Grandma Elleira opened the door, her expression a blend of concern and support. 'Are you ready, Aria?' she asked, her voice gentle but serious. Grandma Elleira had her staff, wand and the book of spells.

'Yes, Grandma,' Aria replied, her voice steady. 'I'm ready.'

They set off together, heading towards the dense forest that bordered their town. The sun was beginning to set, casting long shadows on the path ahead. The air grew cooler, and the sounds of the forest became more pronounced. Aria could feel her nerves tingling, but she stayed close to Grandma Elleira, drawing strength from her presence.

As they walked, Grandma Elleira began to explain more about the vampires and their connection to the full moon. 'Vampires draw their power from the moon's energy,' she said quietly. 'On full moon nights, they are at their strongest. This is why they choose these nights to come out. It's also when they are most likely to be found.

Even though tonight's not a full moon and it's a waning gibbous, the vampires can still draw energy.'

Aria nodded, absorbing the information. She glanced at Elleira, noticing the determination in her eyes. Despite the danger, Elleira was resolute in their mission, and that gave Aria courage.

Every rustle and snap of a twig put Aria on edge, but she kept moving forward, her resolve unwavering. The path ahead was uncertain, but she knew she had to be brave.

The forest was a maze of trees and underbrush, but Grandma Elleira seemed to know the way, guiding them with a sense of purpose.

After what felt like hours of navigating the dense forest, they came to a small clearing. Grandma Elleira stopped and turned to Aria. 'This is it,' she whispered. 'This is where we'll meet the coven. Stay close and be ready.'

Aria's eyes widened. 'This... this is it?'

Grandma nodded. 'This is the gateway to the coven's meeting place. They're expecting us tonight.' She took a deep breath and looked at Aria. 'Stay close to me. The way in can be... disorienting.'

They found a concealed spot behind some thick bushes and settled in, watching and waiting. The anticipation was almost unbearable, but Aria knew this was their best chance to find her brother.

Grandma Elleira's expression softened, a smile spreading across her face. 'That's them,' she whispered, her voice filled with warmth. 'That's my coven,' The witches and wizards approached, their expressions turning from wary to joyous as they recognized Elleira.

Aria watched in awe as Elleira stepped forward, greeted by hugs and laughter. It was a scene of heartfelt reunion, the air filled with a sense of camaraderie and relief.

One of the cloaked figures stepped forward, pulling back their hood to reveal a middle-aged woman with piercing eyes. Her hair was streaked with silver, cascading over her shoulders, adding to her charm of ancient wisdom. Her face was lined with years of experience, but her expression softened the moment she caught sight of Grandma.

'Arielle,' she exclaimed (Aria had momentarily forgotten that she was called Arielle, rather than of Elleira), her voice filled with warmth and joy, cutting through the solemnity of the gathering. The formal air around them seemed to lift, replaced with a sense of reunion. 'We have been expecting you!'

The other cloaked figures began to lower their hoods as well, revealing a mixture of faces—some old, some young—all looking at Grandma with familiarity and affection. A wave of warmth spread through the clearing, and it was as if the entire forest around them breathed a sigh of relief.

Grandma's face lit up with a heartfelt smile that reached her eyes. 'Oh, Persephone,' she responded, her voice breaking the silence of the woods with the intimacy of an old friendship.

Without hesitation, she moved forward, wrapping the woman named Persephone in a tight embrace. The two women held onto each other as if they were reconnecting after ages, their bond immediately evident to all who watched.

One by one, Grandma moved through the small circle of cloaked figures, hugging each of them in turn. Some patted her back warmly, while others squeezed her hands, whispering words of welcome. It was clear that Grandma was more than just a visitor; she was part of this coven, a family within the magical world.

The atmosphere around them grew lighter, filled with the unspoken histories and memories they shared. Aria stood back, observing this tender exchange, her heart swelling with pride and a deep sense of belonging.

Grandma finally turned back to Aria; her eyes gleaming with happiness. 'These are my old friends,' she said, her voice catching slightly. 'My coven. And they are here to help us.' Aria nodded.

She noticed that one of the members who had tangled hair with loosely shackled robes, seemed to be rigid in his position.

'Grandma, who's he?' Aria pointed out to the rigid man. What if he was not welcome here?

Grandma noticed him too. 'Oh Reginald, it's so good to see you too,' exclaimed Grandma.

'Don't talk to me, Arielle.' said the man named Reginald, grumpily. 'Reg,' said Grandma, 'I know that you are upset with me for not turning up for so many years, but please, from now on, I will stay connected to our world too.' Reginald scoffed.

'Thank you everyone,' Grandma replied, inclining her head, 'This is Aria,' introduced Grandma, 'We come seeking guidance and help. We need to enter the vampire world.'

A murmur ran through the gathering as the other wizards exchanged glances. Reginald looked at Aria, his gaze sharp and assessing. 'You bring a mortal with you.'

'She belongs with us,' Grandma said firmly, placing a protective arm around Aria's shoulders. 'And this quest is as much hers as it is mine.'

'Welcome, Aria! It's wonderful to meet you!' chirped the tall witch with silver hair. Aria felt a wave of relief wash over her. Despite the strange and magical circumstances, she felt a sense of belonging among these people.

As the reunion continued, Elleira introduced each member of the coven to Aria. 'This is Persephone.' she said, gesturing to the tall witch who had first greeted her. 'And Phineas.' Grandma pointed to a bald wizard who was bald with a curly moustache, who offered a friendly wink.

'Alice, Arthur, Gabrielle,' she continued, pointing to each one in turn, 'And you know Reginald.'

Aria smiled at each introduction, feeling their warmth surround her like a protective cloak.

After the initial greetings, Elleira gathered the coven around, her demeanour shifting to serious. 'We're here not just for the reunion but also to find Aria's brother, Jayden.' she announced, her voice steady and determined.

Gasps rippled through the group, and the mood quickly turned sombre. 'He was taken by vampires on a full moon night, and we believe they may still be holding him somewhere in the forest.' Elleira continued, her eyes glinting with resolve.

The coven members exchanged serious looks, their expressions hardening with resolve. 'We'll help you,' Persephone said fiercely, her earlier warmth replaced by a warrior's spirit. 'We'll do everything we can to find him.'

'Count on us,' Phineas added, his moustache twitching as he nodded vigorously. 'No vampire stands a chance against our combined strength.'

'Together, we're unstoppable.' Arthur proclaimed, clenching his fists with determination.

Reginald, still crossed-armed, finally spoke up, though his tone was softer. 'Just know, if we're doing this, we're all in. No half-measures.'

Elleira smiled, the tension easing just a little. 'Thank you, Reg. Thank you everyone. Your strength is what we need most right now. We'll meet you all soon.'

'Wait, don't tell me you're leaving,' said the witch named Alice, her expression deflating like a burst balloon.

'I'm sorry, Alice, but we have to go. It was great to see you all after a very long time.' said Grandma. Why did Grandma want to leave, thought Aria. Can't she just stay?

As the coven members nodded and began to disperse, Aria turned to Grandma Elleira. 'Grandma, why did you want to leave?'

'I had to, my dear. All of them were delighted to see me, but I had no other choice as I had to get prepared. It's been a while since I've used magic and if I join them without revising, then I'll probably fail in everything. And besides, your aunt would be worried that you haven't come home yet.' said Grandma seriously.

'Right, as if she cares,' grumbled Aria. 'Grandma, do you really think we can find my brother?'

Elleira knelt, looking directly into Aria's eyes. 'With the strength of this coven, I believe we can overcome any darkness. We'll bring him home, I promise.'

With renewed determination, Aria nodded, ready to face whatever came next.

CHAPTER SIX

Igniting the Spirit

The morning air was still and calm, a stark contrast to the whirlwind of events that had filled Aria's life lately. Exhausted from the excitement and anxiety, Aria had fallen into a deep sleep, hoping for a momentary escape from all the chaos.

But peace was short-lived in her world now.

'Aria, wake up!'

With a groan, Aria slowly tossed and turned. She squinted against the soft morning light streaming through her window, blinking to adjust her eyes. Finally, she focused and saw her aunt standing at the foot of her bed, hands firmly on her hips and a stern look etched on her face.

'Mrs. Miller, what is it?' Aria mumbled, rubbing the sleep from her eyes. It was unusual for her aunt to come to her room to wake her up; she usually relied on her alarm clock to start her day.

'You're going to be late for school if you don't get your legs moving right now.' her aunt replied sharply, urgency lacing her words. 'And it's also better for me when you leave.' she muttered under her breath.

'Wait, I have school today?' Aria asked, ignoring her aunt's grumpiness, her heart racing as reality crashed in. The realisation felt like a bucket of cold water, shaking her fully awake. She struggled to remember what day it was, her mind still foggy.

'Of course you do! Check the day!' her aunt snapped, gesturing impatiently toward the wall calendar beside her desk.

Aria glanced at the calendar on her wall. Her eyes widened in disbelief. 'Oh no! It's Monday? How did I not see this?' Panic bubbled in her chest as memories of unfinished homework and the looming maths test flooded her mind.

'Then you'd better get ready—now!' her aunt barked.

Aria sat up abruptly, the covers slipping off her shoulders as she swung her legs over the side of the bed. 'Right! I'll hurry!' she exclaimed, shaking off the remnants of sleep. She glanced around her messy room, clothes strewn about, and papers piled high on her desk and felt a wave of stress wash over her.

'Don't forget to eat something!' her aunt called over her shoulder as she headed toward the door, her expression etched with annoyance. 'You know how you get when you skip breakfast!'

'Got it!' Aria shouted back, already racing to her closet, her heart pounding as she rifled through her clothes, trying to find something that didn't look like a crumpled disaster.

As she hurriedly dressed, her mind raced with thoughts of the day ahead. Aria tied her shoes as fast as she could, feeling the heat of urgency flood her cheeks. She took a deep breath, pushing aside her lingering thoughts about everything else.

She raced to her school. 'Just in time.' Aria mumbled, for the bell rang just as she stepped into the hallway.

'Late to the test by three minutes, Aria.' said Professor Smith serenely, as he glanced at the clock.

Aria slumped to her seat and started writing the test. Most of the questions were all about x and y in algebra, but since it was an MCQ test, Aria randomly circled the options. She could barely concentrate, her mind drifting to thoughts of her brother and the magical world Grandma Elleira had revealed to her.

'How did you do on the test?' asked one of her classmates as they filed out of the classroom.

'Not half bad.' replied Aria with a shrug, though she knew she hadn't put in her best effort.

The day dragged on, each class feeling longer than the last. She struggled to stay focused, her thoughts a chaotic jumble. Finally, when the last bell of the day rang, she felt a wave of relief wash over her. She quickly gathered her things and headed to Elleira's shop.

The walk to Elleira's shop was a welcome break from the monotony of school.

Elleira looked up from behind the counter, her eyes lighting up with a warm smile. 'Aria, my dear! How was your day?'

'Long,' Aria sighed, dropping her backpack by the door. 'I need to talk, Grandma. Everything feels so overwhelming.'

Elleira nodded understandingly and beckoned her over. 'Let's sit in the back.'

They moved to the small, cosy room behind the shop, where Elleira had a pot of tea ready. Aria sank into a cushioned chair, feeling the weight of the day begin to lift.

'I'm worried about the test,' Aria admitted, taking a sip of the soothing tea. 'But more than that, I can't stop thinking about what you told me. About your coven, about magic, and about my brother.'

Elleira reached across the table and took Aria's hand, giving it a reassuring squeeze. 'It's a lot to take in, I know. But you're not alone in this. We'll find your brother, and I'll help you understand our world.'

'Do you really think we can find him?' Aria asked, her voice tinged with both hope and doubt.

'Yes, I do,' Elleira said firmly. 'And the coven is ready to help. But we need to be prepared. There's much you need to learn, even if you can't use magic yourself.'

Aria nodded, feeling a renewed sense of determination. 'What do I need to do?'

Elleira smiled. 'First, we'll start with the basics. Understanding the magical world and the creatures we might face. Knowledge is your greatest weapon.'

They spent the next few hours talking, Elleira sharing stories and wisdom, teaching Aria about the magical realm that had always been hidden from her. Aria listened intently, absorbing every word. She learned about the coven's history, their battles with vampires, and the intricate network of alliances and enmities that defined their world.

'You might have read that vampires have werewolves as their enemies. However, werewolves are allies of vampires and centaurs are allies of witches and wizards.'

'I see,' said Aria thoughtfully. 'Grandma, I read in the diary that witches existed in the 1800's, so how old are you?'

Grandma chuckled. 'We never keep track of our age. All we know is that Alice is the youngest of all. You see, we're immortal.'

'Wait, so you can't die?' asked Aria.

'We can't die unless vampires kill us,' said Grandma. 'In the last battle, we were harmed fatally, but not killed.'

Aria leaned back, trying to wrap her mind around this new information. 'So, if you're immortal, does that mean you've been fighting these battles for centuries?'

Elleira nodded. 'Yes, our battles with vampires have been ongoing for as long as I can remember.'

Aria felt a surge of admiration for Elleira and the coven. 'It must be exhausting, always having to be on guard.'

'It can be,' Elleira admitted. 'But it's our duty. And now, you are a part of this world, Aria.'

'Even if I can't do magic?' Aria asked, her voice tinged with uncertainty.

'Yes, even if you can't do magic,' Elleira affirmed. 'You have a strength and courage within you that is just as important. And there are other ways to contribute, other skills that can be just as valuable in our fight.'

Aria nodded, feeling a sense of responsibility settle on her shoulders. 'I want to help, Grandma. I want to do whatever I can to find my brother.'

Elleira smiled, her eyes filled with pride. 'I knew you would. And we will find your brother, Aria. Together, we'll face whatever comes our way.'

As they continued to talk, Elleira shared more stories and lessons from her long life, each one revealing a new facet of the magical world. Aria listened intently, feeling more connected to her heritage with each passing moment.

Eventually, Elleira stood up and walked over to a bookshelf lined with ancient tomes and scrolls. She selected a thick, leather-bound book and brought it over to Aria. 'This is the Grimoire of our coven. It contains our history, spells, and knowledge passed down through generations. I want you to read through it.'

Aria took the book reverently, feeling the weight of its importance. 'I will, Grandma. I promise.'

Elleira placed a gentle hand on Aria's shoulder. 'Remember, knowledge is power. And with that power, we will overcome any obstacle.'

'Thank you, Grandma,' Aria said softly as they finished their tea. 'For everything.'

Elleira hugged her tightly. 'We're in this together, Aria. We'll find your brother, and we'll keep our coven safe.'

As Aria left Elleira's shop that evening, Grimoire safely tucked under her arm, she felt a renewed sense of duty. She was no longer just a confused teenager; she was part of the supernatural world, armed with the knowledge and determination to make a difference.

CHAPTER SEVEN

Through the Lenses of Time

A ria walked home with the Grimoire clutched tightly to her chest, feeling a mix of excitement and apprehension. The weight of her new responsibilities pressed down on her, but she was determined to rise to the challenge. She had a brother to find and a magical world to understand.

When she got home, she went straight to her room, locking the door behind her. She placed the Grimoire on her desk and took a deep breath before opening it. The pages were filled with detailed diagrams, spells, and handwritten notes from generations of witches. It was overwhelming, but also fascinating.

Hours passed as she read the text, absorbing as much as she could. She learned about different types of magic, the history of the coven, and the various creatures they had encountered.

Despite her lack of magical abilities, she felt a growing connection to the world Elleira had described.

The next morning, Aria woke up early, eager to continue her studies. She knew that understanding the Grimoire was just the beginning. She needed to be prepared for whatever lay ahead.

At school, she felt a renewed sense of focus. She tackled her classes with determination, knowing that each piece of knowledge could be useful in her quest.

Over the next few weeks, Aria divided her time between school, studying the Grimoire, and spending time with Grandma Elleira. She taught her about the weaknesses of vampires.

'Vampires are typically weaker on new moon nights, and as you might have read in fairy tales, they get burned by the sun. Well, not technically burned,' Grandma corrected, 'More like, their bodies combust and turn to ash. We then ignite those ashes and perform a spell. In this way, our wands will perform magic more efficiently, because the corpse of our enemies remains in our wands, indicating that we've won the battle.'

Even though Aria couldn't perform magic, she absorbed the information like a sponge, knowing that knowledge was her best weapon.

One evening, as she sat in her room, a sharp knock on the door jolted her from her thoughts. She opened it to find her aunt standing there, arms crossed and an unimpressed look on her face.

'Aria, you've been spending an excessive amount of time with Grandma lately,' her aunt stated bluntly. 'Is everything alright?'

Aria hesitated, unsure of how much to disclose. 'Yeah, everything's fine, Mrs. Miller. I've just been learning a lot.' she replied, trying to sound casual.

Her aunt raised an eyebrow, her expression stern. 'Just make sure you don't lose focus on what's important, understood?'

'I won't,' said Aria, though the pressure mounted. 'I'm doing this for him.'

Her aunt nodded curtly, not offering any signs of reassurance. 'Just keep that in mind. No more distractions.'

'I will,' Aria said, feeling a surge of determination, but the weight of her aunt's disapproval lingered heavily in the air.

One day, Grandma called Aria to her chamber. The room was dimly lit, with candles flickering around, casting shadows on the old, dusty tomes and ancient artefacts scattered about. Elleira stood by the window, her face etched with worry as she gazed out at the twilight sky.

'Grandma, is everything alright? You seem to be worried.' Aria asked, concerned.

Elleira turned slowly, her eyes reflecting a depth of emotion that Aria rarely saw. She motioned for Aria to sit down in one of the plush chairs near the hearth.

'Oh, my dear,' Elleira began, 'You see, I've been getting this strange instinct that your brother knew something about this world, you know, about the world of witches, wizards and vampires before he was taken away. And my instinct is pretty much right most of the time.'

Aria felt a chill run down her spine. 'You mean, he might have been aware of the magical world? But how?'

Elleira nodded, her expression grave. 'Yes, Aria. I believe he may have discovered a secret or something that drew the attention of the vampires. They must have seen him as a threat or as someone who could expose their plans.'

'But why wouldn't he have told us?' Aria asked, her voice trembling. 'Why keep it a secret?'

'Fear, perhaps,' Elleira suggested gently. 'Or maybe he didn't fully understand what he had found. Sometimes, knowledge can be a heavy burden, especially for someone so young.'

Aria clenched her fists, feeling a mix of anger and helplessness. 'We have to find him, Grandma. We need to know what he knew before he was taken away. It could be the key to bringing him back.'

Elleira reached out and took Aria's hand, squeezing it reassuringly. 'We will, my dear. But we must be cautious. If the vampires took him because of what he knew, they won't let him go easily.'

'So, what can we do?' asked Aria.

'There's one thing that's on my mind right now. It might sound strange, but that's the only way for now.'

'What is it?' asked Aria. The only thing that mattered the most was her brother, not her safety.

'Can I cast a spell on you?' asked Grandma.

'What?' Aria was puzzled. She wasn't able to see where the conversation was leading to.

'You know, I can cast a spell that can bring back your memories of the past, that is, you can see them more clearly. However, the downside is that you'll be awake in the past, but not in the present.'

Aria found it still confusing. 'How is bringing back my memories and allowing me to see them more clearly going to help in finding my brother?'

'You might see some clues about your brother's behaviour. Are you sure you can take up this?'

'Yes, Grandma, I am,' said Aria, 'But how can we bring back our memories?'

'Under this spell, if you focus on one item, then you will see memories that you have shared with your brother related to that item. For example, if you had earlier fought about a pen, and if you focus on that same exact pen now, then memories, including the one which you have fought with your brother, will cloud your vision and you won't be able to focus on the present world. In fact, you will sleep in the present world.'

'For how long will we sleep, Grandma?'

'For a minute of memories, you will be in a slumber of one hour in the present world.'

'One hour?' asked Aria, surprised.

'Yes, dear,' Grandma confirmed. 'Time works differently with this spell. It makes you fully experience the emotions and events tied to those memories. This can be very confusing. When you wake up, it will feel like you just experienced those moments again. That's why this spell is powerful but also dangerous. Spending too much time in the past means losing time in the present. Use it carefully and only when you really need to.'

Aria nodded thoughtfully, processing Grandma's warning. The idea of experiencing memories intrigued her, but the cost was daunting.

'Is there a way to control which memories we see?' Aria asked, her curiosity piqued.

Grandma shook her head gently. 'No, the spell draws out whatever memories are most strongly tied to the item you're focusing on. You can't pick and choose. That's part of what makes it so unpredictable.'

'Grandma,' Aria asked, 'Can you show me how the spell works?'

Grandma looked at her with a mix of concern and affection. 'Are you sure, Aria? This is not something to take lightly.'

'I'm sure,' Aria said, determined.

'Very well,' said Elleira, 'Sit down and close your eyes. I will cast the spell on you.'

Aria settled into a comfortable position and closed her eyes, taking a deep breath. Grandma took out her wand and pointed it to aria. Then, there was silence. Grandma was concentrating and was reciting the spell in her mind. Aria felt a warm, tingling sensation.

'Open your eyes,' said Grandma softly.

Aria opened her eyes and expected something unusual, but she saw only the same dimly lit room and Elleira in front of her.

'Wait, that's it?'

Grandma nodded.

'Now what?' asked Aria.

'Go home and sleep. Wake up early in the morning because you'll have to sleep *again* by focusing on an item. I'm asking you to sleep tonight because this spell will be effective only when the sun rises in the morning.'

'Alright, Grandma,' said Aria, 'Goodnight.'

'Goodnight, my dear.'

Aria walked to her home. The walk was slow-paced, and the thought of seeing her brother again in memories more clearly made Aria both ecstatic and scared. Ecstatic, because Aria had not been with her brother for nearly one whole month. Scared, because of what she might see.

What if these memories contained something upsetting, something she wasn't prepared or meant to see? What if her brother will not be the same ever again?

When Aria got home, she went straight to her room and locked the door. She lay down on her bed, feeling the familiar comfort. Her eyelids began to droop as the weight of the day's emotions lifted from her shoulders. The heavy burden she had been carrying—the mix of excitement and fear about her memories of her brother—started to ease. For the first time in what felt like ages, she felt calm. Finally, she began to drift off to sleep.

The next day, Aria woke up and went to school. They told the scores of the algebra test Aria had attended terribly.

'Adaline, ninety-four percent. Well done,' called out Professor Smith, 'Alastria, sixty-two percent. Aria, sixty-seven percent. Cornelia, eighty-five percent,' And he droned on.

Aria shoved her test paper inside her bag. She hadn't studied for the test, and she wouldn't keep that as the top priority either. Finding her lost brother was more important than anything else.

Aria was not looking forward to the next science class. Her teacher would ask questions about fungi and its benefits, and Aria hadn't touched her science book for three weeks straight.

'Alright class, so what are the most pivotal and significant benefits of fungi? You,' pointed out Professor Loomy to a boy named Jamison, who was fidgeting with his pen.

Jamison stood up. 'Erm, it improves in nutrient cycling?'

'And?' Professor Loomy nudged the poor boy to proceed.

'Er,' Jamison hesitated. Clearly, he didn't pay attention to class, and Professor Loomy noticed it too.

'I spent an entire hour—' barked Professor Loomy, Aria knew that it wasn't an hour but only fifteen minutes '— and all you say, young man, is one out of fourteen benefits given in the textbook,' barked Professor Loomy, 'Detention for you, Mr. Jamison.' Poor Jamison slumped back into his chair and sighed, clearly showing an expression of exhaustion.

Aria managed to survive the entire science period. Professor Loomy never really liked Aria much, and Aria was grateful for *that*.

She then rushed to Professor Johnson's class, which Aria found to be a perfect time to doze off. She slumped on the desk, and pretended to take notes, while her thoughts were astray. She fiddled with her pen and noticed a J scrawled on the top of the pen. Just then, a cosy atmosphere was created that lulled her eyelids heavier and heavier.

'Wait,' a voice called out, breaking through the haze of her thoughts.

Aria wheeled around in surprise, finding herself face-to-face with her younger self and her brother. They looked so carefree, full of life. Little Aria wore a frayed nightgown, her hair a wild tangle that resembled a bush, while Jayden was equally messy, his short jet-black hair framing his cherubic face. In that moment, she felt a pang of regret for not appreciating his youthful spirit back then.

'What?' asked little Aria, confusion etched on her face.

'How are you going to name this? I tried to use a pen on this pen, but it got smudged, and now there's ink everywhere.' little Jayden explained, holding the pen with an innocent pout. Hearing his voice again was like a warm embrace, flooding Aria with nostalgia.

'With a permanent marker! Here,' said younger Aria, eagerly handing him her favourite marker. 'This will keep your name on the pen for good. There's not much space, so just write your initial.'

'Thank you, sissy! You're the best!' Jayden beamed, his eyes sparkling with joy.

'Not to mention you!' younger Aria giggled back, their bond evident in their playful exchange.

As Aria's eyes brimmed with tears, memories cascading like a gentle rain, an unfamiliar voice suddenly pierced through the moment, pulling her back to reality.

'Aria, wake up!' shouted Professor Johnson, his voice firm yet concerned.

Aria's eyes snapped open, her heart racing as she realised the entire class was gathered around her, watching with a mix of worry and curiosity.

'Is everything alright? You seem out of sorts today. Do you want to go to the first aid room?' Professor Johnson asked, his eyebrow furrowed with concern.

'First aid? Why?' Aria replied, confusion mingling with embarrassment.

'Well, you haven't been yourself lately, and your grades are slipping.' Professor Johnson continued, his tone gentle but serious.

'I'm fine, Professor Johnson,' Aria said hastily, trying to brush off her worries. 'It's just—I haven't been getting good sleep the past few days because I've been up all-night researching.'

'Researching? So, no late movie nights?' Professor Johnson quipped, a hint of humour in his voice.

Aria shook her head. Watching movies was the very last thing on her mind when she was focused on finding her brother.

'Very well, Aria. Just don't let me catch you falling asleep in class again. Students,' Professor Johnson called, giving the class a nod before returning to her lecture, leaving Aria feeling a mix of relief and lingering sadness.

As soon as school ended, Aria rushed to Elleira's shop to tell her about what happened in school.

Aria told the entire story of how she slept in class and visited a memory.

'That's interesting. Did you find anything peculiar?' asked Elleira after she heard Aria's tale.

'Not really. All we did was to name a pen with my brother's initial with a permanent marker.'

Aria was focused on a random object lying on the table. It was a tiny figurine, neatly engraved with feathers and was carved with intricate symbols. She believed that she saw it somewhere but couldn't recollect where.

Suddenly, Aria felt the familiar sensation of swooping into the past.

'Can we buy this?' said the little Aria, holding a figurine in a supermarket.

The much older Aria felt a sensation of being woken up.

Aria's eyes flew open. She saw Grandma, whose expression was worried.

'Did I just sleep?' asked Aria, waking up in the present world.

'You did, for a couple of minutes.' replied Elleira.

'Grandma, what's that?' asked Aria, pointing to the figurine.

'Oh, you gave me that, remember?' said Grandma, 'When you were about six years old, you and your brother gave me the figurine as a birthday gift.'

'Oh,' said Aria, 'But why would the spell show me and my brother buying a figurine?'

'Maybe, it's related to me. You know, because I am a witch.'

'You mean to say that the memory with the pen was also supposed to be related to witches?' asked Aria.

'I guess so,' said Grandma thoughtfully. 'Wait, which pen are you talking about?'

Aria opened the zipper and dug through the bag. She fumbled upon the black pen.

'Your brother showed me this pen,' said Grandma, holding the pen in her hands, 'Because you had given him as a gift for getting good grades.'

'Wait, really?' asked Aria. Grandma nodded.

'Hmm,' said Grandma Elleira thoughtfully. 'I thought that the spell was supposed to wear off after you revisit a particular number of memories.'

Aria saw the magical Grimoire lying on the table with its pages open. She took the Grimoire in her hands and absent-mindedly turned to the front page. Then, Aria felt herself slumping onto the desk.

A memory came rushing back with vivid clarity. She could see their younger selves, hear their raised voices, and feel the tension between them.

Suddenly, the memory expanded, drawing her into it completely. She was no longer just remembering; she was there, experiencing it. She felt the frustration and anger and the heat of the argument.

They were arguing about a teddy bear.

The experience was overwhelming. Aria felt every emotion as if it were happening in real time. She lost track of everything else, completely immersed in the memory.

In the midst of the memory, something strange happened. Aria noticed her brother, who seemed to be hiding something from her. She saw him discovering an old, dusty book, which looked like...the Grimoire.

His eyes widened with excitement and fear as he flipped through the pages. He looked around cautiously, making sure no one was watching, and then quickly hid the book back where he found it, acting as if nothing had happened.

Aria's mind raced. Why hadn't her brother told her about the Grimoire? What kind of spells did it contain back then?

The memory continued, but now with a new layer of mystery. She saw them arguing over a teddy bear again, but her brother's secret knowledge of the magic book added a new dimension to the scene.

After what felt like an eternity, the memory began to fade. Aria felt herself being pulled back, the sensations slowly dissipating until she was once again aware of the present.

She opened her eyes to find Grandma watching over her with concern.

'How long was I out?' Aria asked, her voice shaky. She saw the night sky, the stars glinting above.

'Three hours,' Grandma replied softly. 'You experienced three minutes of memories.'

Aria sat up slowly, her head spinning. 'It felt so real. Like I was really there. And... I saw something strange,' Aria hesitated, 'My brother—he found the Grimoire and hid it from me.'

Grandma's eyes widened slightly. 'The Grimoire? But, how? Your brother was never prone to magic, neither were you, but how is it that he had a magical book? And the book was also under my protection.'

'I—don't know,' Aria felt ashamed to not know about her own brother.

'That's curious. It seems your brother has secrets of his own. You must be careful, Aria. Magic can be powerful, but it can also be dangerous, especially if not handled properly.'

Aria nodded, feeling a newfound respect for the spell and the memories it could unlock. 'I understand, Grandma. I'll be careful.'

Grandma smiled and hugged her tightly. 'That's all I ask, dear. Remember, the past is important, but it's the present where we truly live.'

Aria nodded thoughtfully, now determined to find out more about her brother's discovery and why he had kept it from her.

Aria looked into Grandma's eyes, seeing the determination there. 'What do we do now?'

'We need to dig deeper,' Elleira said firmly. 'We need to look for any clues he might have left behind. His room, his belongings—anything that could give us a hint. And we need to be prepared for what we might find.'

Aria nodded, feeling a surge of resolve. 'I'll start searching his room tonight. There has to be something we missed.'

'The spell must wear off now, because we've discovered something major.'

As they made their plans, Aria couldn't shake the feeling that time was running out. She had to find her brother and uncover the secrets he had stumbled upon. The safety of the coven depended on it.

That night, as Aria combed through her brother's room, she felt a sense of urgency. She searched every nook and cranny, looking for anything out of the ordinary. Finally, hidden beneath a loose floorboard, she found an old leather-bound journal. Her hands trembled as she opened it, revealing pages filled with her brother's handwriting.

As Aria read through his entries, she stumbled upon a memory from their eighth birthday.

The first line written was enough for Aria to know that it was truly her brother.

CHAPTER EIGHT

The Hidden Reality

My sister is the best. She gave me a toy and a beautiful pen to write for my seventh birthday. She also gave me my favourite chocolate- Banana Toffees.

I gave my sister a ring for her seventh birthday — which was also on the same day because we are twins. How cool is THAT? Anyways, the ring which I gave was no ordinary ring — it was made from paper. And guess who made it? Me!

Me, my sister and my family cut a strawberry-chocolate cake because I like strawberries, and my sister likes chocolate. The icing read: 'Happy B'day to the most loved ones: Aria and Jay'. My sissy calls me Jay, she tells me that it's too long to pronounce – and I wonder, what's long to pronounce? It's just Jay-den, two syllables. It's not like she's trying to pronounce the world's longest word.

Anyways, our family surprised us by taking us to a movie which me and Aria begged for!

We also went to Grandma Elleira's shop, who gave a pencil case to each one of us. Sissy got the one with red colour, while I got the one with blue colour. Then, Grandma asked us to stay for dinner, but we had to go because our homework was not done.

I just want to say that this was one of my best days EVER 'cause I got to spend time with my family!

Reading this brought tears to Aria's eyes. Jayden cherished their time together so deeply, and his words remind her of how special their bond was.

As Aria continued to read through Jayden's diary, she felt a bittersweet mix of joy and sorrow. Each entry was a window into her brother's world, filled with love and excitement. One particular entry caught her attention, which brought her back a flood of memories.

Another unforgettable day with Aria. We decided to have an adventure in the backyard, pretending we were explorers in a jungle. Aria led the way, and I followed, trusting her completely. We discovered our 'hidden treasures', which were shiny rocks. Aria said we should keep them in a special box, so we could remember our adventure forever.

We also had our secret hideout under the old oak tree, where we whispered our dreams and plans. Aria said she wanted to be an artist, and I told her I wanted to be a writer, sharing our stories with everyone. We promised to support each other no matter what.

In the evening, we helped Mom bake cookies. Aria was in charge of decorating, and she made each cookie look like a little piece of art. I tried my best to make mine look good too, but they were nothing compared to Aria's masterpieces. She always knew how to make everything more beautiful.

Before bed, we read our favourite book together. Aria did the voices, making the characters come to life. I laughed so hard at her silly impressions, and she joined in, her laughter echoing through the room. It was moments like these that I cherished the most, the simple, joyful times we shared.

> Every time I write this, I always think about how lucky I am to have a sister like Aria. She makes every day brighter, and I can't wait to see what adventures we will have tomorrow.

His entries reminded Aria of the bond they had, a bond that death could never break. She vowed to keep his memory alive, to cherish their adventures, and to continue living in a way that would make him proud.

With a heavy heart, she tucked the diary away, knowing that Jayden's spirit would always be with her. He was Aria's brother, twin, and her best friend, and his love would guide Aria through the rest of her journey to finding her brother.

The next day, Aria woke up with a heavy heart but felt an urge to share Jayden's beautiful memories with Grandma Elleira. She shoved the diary in her bag, and she went to Elleira's shop in the morning, only to find Grandma Elleira, not knitting this time, but going through some books. Aria was sure that they had to do something with magic.

'Hello, Grandma,' said Aria as she approached Grandma.

'Aria! Hello,' said Grandma, with a peculiar enthusiasm, 'I was just looking through the Grimoire about the spell which I casted on you. I had a sudden doubt if I had done something wrong.'

'Oh, I see.' said Aria, as she dragged a chair and sat near Elleira.

'In the Grimoire, the language is sort of twisted to tell you the description of the spell, you know, in the form of *riddles*. And I found the riddle of the spell. Look,' added Elleira.

The pages of the book were vintage, yet in a decent condition. Aria looked closely at the riddle Elleira was pointing at.

I bring the past to light so clear,
Focus on an item and memories appear.
But as you glimpse, you'll fall asleep,
An hour lost for each minute you keep.

What am I, who trades the now for then?

'Wow, I never knew that there was so much in magic. Well, guess I have a lot to learn,' said Aria to herself, 'But why is it given in the form of riddles, Grandma?' asked

Aria, as she plainly wondered that they could have been given in normal language itself.

'Well, didn't you read in Maria's diary that we like to keep everything a secret and show everything in puzzles?' asked Grandma.

'Oh, right. I forgot about that.' said Aria, as she faintly recalled reading it in Maria's diary.

'Yeah, well I guess that puts an end to our problems. For now, of course.' added Grandma, as she saw the tentative look in Aria's eyes.

'Er, well not quite.' said Aria, as she opened her bag and fumbled on her brother's diary.

'Yesterday, you told me to search his room and when I did, I found *this.*' said Aria, as she handed the diary to Elleira.

Grandma flicked the diary open and traced her fingers along Jayden's handwriting.

'Where did you find this?' asked Elleira, her eyes still glued to the diary.

'Hidden beneath a loose floorboard.' replied Aria.

'Well, then it's obvious that he would not have wanted anybody to know about this.' said Grandma.

'Not even to his own sister?' asked Aria, as she suddenly felt a pang of ache over her.

Grandma looked up and found tears streaming down through Aria's heart-shaped face.

'My dear,' said Grandma, as she closed the book and went to hug her, wrapping her arms around Aria, 'it's not that Jayden didn't want you to know. Sometimes people keep their deepest thoughts and feelings hidden, even from the ones they love most. It doesn't mean he didn't care about you; in fact, it often means the opposite.'

Aria looked up, her eyes glistening with tears. 'But why would he hide something like this from me?'

Grandma Elleira sighed gently. 'Jayden might have kept this diary secret to protect you from his own uncertainties. Maybe he wanted to keep your memories of him unstained by whatever he was going through. It's not always easy to share everything, especially when you're struggling with something inside.'

Aria sniffled, trying to hold back more tears. 'I just miss him so much, and finding this diary felt like I still had a piece of him. But knowing he hid it . . . it hurts.'

'I know, sweetheart,' said Grandma, pulling back slightly to look into her eyes. 'But remember, everyone has their own way of dealing with things. This diary is a special glimpse into his heart, a chance to connect with him in a new way, even if he didn't intend for you to find it.'

Aria nodded slowly, understanding starting to dawn on her. 'It's just hard to accept that there's so much I'll never know about him now.'

'That's true,' Grandma Elleira agreed, her eyes filled with understanding. 'But that's what makes memories and love so precious. The mysteries, the unknown parts, are all part of the journey. And with a little magic, we can cherish and remember the best parts, even if we can't fully grasp the whole story.'

Aria took a deep breath, feeling a small sense of peace. She glanced at the diary in Elleira's hands. 'Do you think there's more magic in this book, Grandma? Something that could help me understand him better?'

Grandma Elleira smiled gently and opened the diary to the first page. 'Magic isn't just about spells, Aria. It's about the connections we make and the love we share. Let's explore this together. We might find more than just words on a page. We might perhaps discover even some magic he left behind for us to find. C'mon, have a seat and we'll look through it.'

'I've looked at most of it by last night, actually.' said Aria, as she sat beside Grandma Elleira.

'I *totally* didn't expect that.' said Grandma with amusement. Aria chuckled.

They went through the pages one by one, and Aria cherished every moment of it. As time passed by, Aria felt her stomach grumbling. She looked at the time. It was three-thirty in the afternoon. Grandma had too apparently noticed Aria, for she had slowly shifted away from her chair.

'Hungry?' asked Grandma Elleira.

'Yeah.' replied Aria.

'I got that all the time when I was a kid.' said Grandma.

'Right. I'll probably go to my house and just grab something to eat.' said Aria, as she got up from her chair.

'What do you think you're doing, young girl?' asked Grandma, 'This might just be a shop, but it has a whole pantry in there. C'mon, follow me. Besides you'll get better food here,' said Grandma, winking one of her eyes.

Aria followed Grandma to the back door, and she noticed her taking out her wand.

'You're going to magic food?' asked Aria incredulously.

'Yep,' said Grandma, 'Which food do you like the most? Forgive me, for I don't really have enough time to ask about your preferences.' said Grandma, chuckling.

'I honestly don't mind. At this rate, I'd have anything that's on the plate.'

'Oh well, then let me just give you a bit of everything.'

'Erm, sure.' said Aria.

Grandma closed her eyes for a fraction of second and out of nowhere, an entire plate of food landed on the table nearby. The plate had some fruits, a hamburger, a pizza, a burrito, a couple of sandwiches, some sausages and fries with ketchup.

'Wow,' remarked Aria, 'That's a lot to eat, Grandma. I love magic.'

'Me too,' said Elleira as Aria started to much on the apple, 'We'll take this food inside, so that we can look through the diary and eat.'

They went back to the counter and sat down, the heavy old book lying open in front of them, its pages yellowed with age and filled with strange symbols and ancient text.

Elleira flipped through the brittle pages, each one feeling like it could crumble under her fingers. As they reached the twenty-third page, Grandma's hand suddenly stilled, her eyes narrowing.

Aria looked up, sensing the shift in Elleira's mood. 'What is it, Grandma?' she asked, her voice tinged with concern.

Grandma didn't immediately answer. Her gaze was fixed on a symbol etched onto the page, her brow furrowing as though she had stumbled upon something unexpected, something dangerous. 'This symbol,' Grandma whispered, leaning closer, her voice low and tense.

'What about it?' Aria pressed, her worry deepening. Her heart began to race as she tried to make sense of the cryptic markings, but they meant nothing to her.

'It's of—' Grandma's voice trailed off, and the pause felt like an eternity to Aria, her stomach knotting with anxiety.

'Of what, Grandma?' Aria asked again, more insistent now, feeling the weight of Grandma Elleira's hesitation like a growing storm.

'—of vampires.' Grandma finally said, her voice barely above a whisper, but the words hit Aria like a physical blow.

Aria's breath caught in her throat, and for a moment, she felt as though the world had tipped sideways. 'Vampires?' she echoed, her voice small and disbelieving. Her skin prickled with unease, and she could almost feel the darkness that this word conjured, the danger it signified.

'Yes,' Grandma confirmed grimly, her eyes sharp with knowledge. 'Look closely.'

Aria leaned in, her face inches from the page now, staring hard at the intricate symbol Elleira was pointing to. It was delicate yet menacing, the sharp lines weaving together in a way that sent a shiver down her spine. The more she looked, the more ominous it became. There was no mistaking it—this symbol carried a warning, an ancient one.

'Here, let me show you how.' Grandma said, her voice calm but with an underlying intensity that commanded attention. She reached over to the counter, grabbing a nearby piece of paper and a pen with swift movements.

Without hesitation, she pressed the tip of the pen against the paper, her hand moving with practised ease. Each stroke was deliberate, as though she had done this a thousand times before. Her eyes focused sharply on the page, and the faint scratching sound of the pen filled the silence.

'Watch closely,' she said, glancing briefly at Aria to ensure she was paying attention. Grandma's hand moved in fluid, precise motions.

'There's a 'V',' said Grandma as she drew a large 'V' on the paper. Then, turning the paper upside down, she added a line across the 'V'. 'Here's an 'A'.'

She flipped the paper back and drew two diagonal lines from the edges of the 'V'. 'That's an 'M',' she explained, her hand steady as she sketched. Next, she added what looked like a semicircle attached to one of the lines. 'Now that's a 'P',' she continued, tracing the outline of the semicircle and the line.

"'I,' she said, as she made a short stroke above the 'A'. Then, with a swift movement, she drew a diagonal line from the point of the semicircle, transforming it into an 'R'. 'There's your 'R'.'

"'E,' Grandma said, as she drew a small line at the top of the 'V', connecting it to complete the letter. 'And that's an 'S',' she added, forming the letter 'S' in the loop of the 'P'.

'V—A—M—P—I—R—E—S,' said Grandma Elleira, tracing over each letter once more, her eyes serious as the word took shape before Aria.

'Wow, Grandma, that's incredible!' exclaimed Aria, her eyes wide with amazement.

Grandma Elleira gave a small smile, her expression serious despite the praise. 'Yes, it is. Vampires, like us, enjoy having their secrets—symbols, codes, hidden messages that often go unnoticed by anyone outside their world. The curious part is that no one in our coven was able to decipher this symbol. For centuries, it remained a mystery. But my friend Alice, bless her soul, uncovered its meaning about seven decades ago.' Grandma explained, her tone both proud and cautious.

'Seven?' Aria repeated, eyes narrowing. 'That's... recent for you, right? I mean, given that you're, you know, immortal and all.'

'Yes,' Grandma nodded, 'But the real mystery here is why that symbol is in your brother's diary. Did he draw it intentionally, or was it an accident?'

'Or,' Aria interjected, 'Did someone else come into his room, take his diary, and draw it?' Her voice took on a sharper edge, adding another layer to the unfolding puzzle.

'What we know for certain is that Jayden knew something about vampires.' Grandma said, her voice firm with conviction. 'And there's no denying it.'

'Certainly.' Aria agreed, though deep down, accepting that truth felt impossible.

'It also means your brother isn't dead—yet.' Grandma added quickly, her words slicing through the air.

'What?' Aria's heart skipped a beat. 'How are you sure that he's not dead?'

'Now we know that your brother's sudden disappearance has got to do something with vampires, and vampires just don't steal people for fun. They might steal for two reasons— either the victim has information that can help the vampires, or the victim has information that could harm them, although, I highly doubt your brother was taken for the second reason.'

'But why him?' Aria's voice trembled with frustration. 'Why my brother? Why not someone else?'

'I don't have a concrete answer to that,' Grandma admitted, her face grave. 'Perhaps he stumbled upon something they wanted. Vampires are not exactly known for their kindness, nor for asking politely.'

Aria frowned, her mind racing. 'But you still haven't explained how you know he's not dead.'

Grandma sighed, her expression softening. 'As I've told you before, my instincts are rarely wrong. The coven has trusted my intuition many times over the years. I have a... knack for sensing these things.'

'But you didn't have much luck with Maria.' Aria murmured, her voice filled with both hesitation and sadness.

'Sweetheart,' Grandma's tone softened but held firm resolve. 'We must hold onto hope. If you believe Jayden is still alive, then that belief will drive you to find him. If you don't... well, you'd be consumed by guilt, thinking it was all your fault. Trust your hope, Aria. That's what keeps us going. Believe in your search, and in your brother.'

'Thank you, Grandma,' Aria murmured, her voice barely above a whisper, yet it carried the weight of all the emotion she had been holding in.

Grandma studied her for a moment, her sharp eyes softening ever so slightly. 'We don't have time to waste,' she said, her voice steady but urgent. 'Now,' Grandma asked, the urgency returning to her voice, 'Where do we begin?'

Aria paused for a second, taking in the enormity of the situation. There were so many unanswered questions, so much they didn't know.

'Anywhere, really,' said Aria, her determination returning. 'But maybe start by casting a spell on me.'

CHAPTER NINE

Veiled in Memory

Grandma raised one of her eyebrows and showed a look of confusion. 'Erm, what spell?' she asked hesitantly.

'Is there a spell to uncover secrets?' asked Aria.

'Unfortunately, no. If there were, I would have known about Maria's intentions long ago.' replied Elleira.

'Right, well, is there anything close to that?'

'Hmm, let me check the Grimoire.' Elleira said, reaching for the tattered brown book.

Grandma and Aria sat down at the pale vintage desk and went through the Grimoire again. As they went through the Grimoire, Aria saw various spells, 'Forecasting

Shadows,' 'Memory Dust,' The one they had tried. One particular title intrigued her, 'Memory Retrieval Charm'.

'Grandma, hang on.' said Aria, stopping her from turning to the next page. Grandma's eyes focused on the open page.

'Memory Retrieval Charm?' she asked, her tone curious.

'What does it do?' Aria inquired, thinking that the downside couldn't be that bad.

'Well, I didn't want you to face any downsides with the spells, which is why I didn't choose this one initially. But do you want to try it?' Grandma replied.

'If it's the only way to make things faster, then I'll do it. But let's check the downside first.' Aria insisted.

They both leaned closer to the page, and there it was—the essential warning of the spell.

Memory Retrieval Charm

Incantation: Memoria Revoca'

I am the key to what's concealed,
A portal where the past is revealed.

*What once was hidden, now revealed,
Yet not all wounds have fully healed.*

*Seek the truth, but pay the toll,
For I may uncover more than your goal.
Beware the shadows I unbind,
For not all that's found will be kind.*

*Use me wisely, as when the flood becomes too strong,
Past and present blend too long.
Clarity fades, fragments remain,
Leaving you in a maze of strain.*

'That's a long riddle,' sighed Aria. 'But what does it mean, Grandma?'

Grandma chuckled softly, but there was a serious undertone in her voice. 'It's not just a riddle, Aria. It's a warning.'

'A warning? About what?' asked Aria, leaning in closer.

'This spell,' Grandma said, tapping the page gently, 'it lets you dig into your memories—those that have been lost or hidden. But memories aren't always simple. Some of them are buried deep because they're too painful to keep on the surface.'

Aria's curiosity was now mixed with a hint of worry. 'So, if I use this spell, I might remember things I don't want to? Like, bad things?'

'Exactly,' Grandma replied, her tone serious. 'It's like opening a door. You might be looking for something specific, but other things could come through too—things you've forgotten for a reason. The spell doesn't just bring back the one memory you're searching for. It can unlock others as well.'

Aria's eyes narrowed as she tried to grasp the full meaning. 'So, it's not just a matter of remembering. It's about dealing with whatever comes up, even if I don't want to?'

Grandma nodded. 'Yes. And sometimes, too many memories at once can overwhelm you. It can blur the lines between what's happening now and what happened in the past. That's what the riddle means when it talks about 'past and present blend too long'.'

'Will this spell end quickly, Grandma? I won't be stuck awake for hours, right?' Aria asked, a hint of nervousness creeping into her voice.

'The riddle doesn't mention anything like that, so I'd say no.' Grandma replied with a reassuring smile.

Aria took a deep breath and nodded. 'Alright then, I'm ready now, Grandma.' she said, her voice firm with determination.

'Wait, what do you mean by 'now'?' asked Elleira, a tinge of panic in her voice. Grandma sighed as Aria gave her a doubting look. 'Right, are you sure that you want to do this, Aria? Remember, some choices can be changed, while others cannot.'

'I'm absolutely sure, Grandma.' said Aria, with a sense of resolve.

'Well then,' said Grandma as she drew out her wand, 'close your eyes and I'll do the incantation.'

Aria shut her eyes, feeling the world spin around her. Doubts crept in—had she made the right decision? Should she really let Grandma cast this spell on her?

Just as she was about to open her eyes and tell Grandma she wasn't sure about this, she heard Grandma's clear voice.

'Memoria Revoca!' said Grandma.

Aria felt a sudden rush, as if she were being pulled through a tunnel of swirling lights and shadows. The sensation was overwhelming—both exhilarating and terrifying.

Memories, long forgotten or buried deep, began to flicker in her mind like distant stars coming into view. She saw flashes of moments from her childhood, snippets of conversations with her brother, faces of people she hadn't thought about in years.

But then, the warmth of those memories began to shift. The light grew dimmer, the images more fragmented, and suddenly, Aria was forced into memories she hadn't intended to revisit—ones that were painful, even haunting.

Aria was suddenly pulled into the most painful memory of her life.

'Here, I made something for you.' said the little Jayden, as he fumbled upon a bracelet in his pocket.

'Aww, thank you, Jay. You didn't have to waste all your time making this while you're supposed to be preparing for the science exam.' said Aria, chuckling, as she reached out her hand for the bracelet.

'Anything for you, sissy,' said Jayden, 'We're not going to live forever or be immortal like the—' paused Jayden, then continued, 'Well, we should enjoy the present as much as we can, right? What's a little science exam compared to that?' said Jayden, as he tried to fasten the bracelet around her wrist. Aria chuckled, touched by his gesture.

However, little Jayden accidentally dropped his beautiful orange bracelet with a silver half-pendant. 'I'm sorry, Aria,' said Jayden, as Aria bent down to pick the bracelet. Just then, a chilling sound filled the air. As Aria looked up, she saw her brother being dragged away into the Midnight Woods, though back then Aria wasn't familiar with the name.

But then, Aria found out why she thought in the first place that it wasn't an 'animal' which took away her brother, because she had seen a long, chalky white hand creeping around the collar of her brother's shirt as he was dragged away. It wasn't any ordinary animal.

It was a vampire.

Tears streamed down through Aria's face. In the midst of her anguish, she heard a voice from the present, cutting through the haze of the past. She knew whose voice it was.

'Grandma!' Aria's voice cracked with desperation; her eyes still tightly shut. 'I... I don't want to see this anymore!'

But Grandma's voice came through, calm yet tinged with concern. 'Focus, Aria. You're stronger than this. Remember why you started. Push through the pain and find the memory you need.'

'I think I already found what I needed,' Aria said softly, opening her eyes. The dim, warm light of the room brought Aria back to the present. The effect of the spell was instantaneous, for Aria found it hard to distinguish between the past and the present—as though they both had converged together.

'Well, how are you holding up?' asked Grandma, as her gaze was focused on Aria, with a look of concern and care.

'It was—' Aria struggled to find the right word, '—intense. I thought that the spell was going to show me my happy memories, well it first did, I don't exactly know what happened, but the spell changed its path to the sad ones. I didn't know how to avoid it, so I faced it. But, somehow, it showed me the memory I never wanted to revisit again. The one memory I dreaded of.'

'So, you mean to say, that it targeted your weakness?' asked Elleira curiously.

'I think it did,' replied Aria, 'I'm not sure though.'

'What did you see?' asked Grandma.

'Well, what do you think I saw?' asked Aria.

A sense of realisation crossed Elleira's face, 'The one with your brother, right? You know that he was dragged to the woods?' asked Grandma doubtfully.

Aria nodded her head as though she were deeply impacted by the memory. If only she had made a move to stop him from being taken and instead put herself forward as the sacrifice her brother had made. If only she had caught the bracelet before it fell to the ground... or stopped him from going to the forest in the first place...

Just then, Aria had the wildest idea ever.

'Grandma, is there a spell in the Grimoire for time travelling?'

'I—' hesitated Grandma, 'Look, darling, I deeply understand your concern and troubles, but meddling with time is one of the most common mistakes wizards have made in their lives. It has changed their lives. But what do you want to change in the past?' asked Grandma, for she did not have the faintest idea where this conversation was leading to.

'I want my brother to stop going to the forest in the past,' said Aria, 'In that way, he would have not gone to the forest in the first place, the vampires wouldn't have been able to grab him, and we would lead a normal, happy life.'

Grandma listened to Aria intently and shook her head slightly, 'That's not how it works dear. You're thinking of avoiding the situation, but your brother would have had other plans. He would have thought of facing it someday if not on that day. The past holds secrets better left untouched—meddling with it can create more chaos than clarity.'

'But it's worth giving it a try, right?' said Aria, in an attempt to convince Elleira, 'I mean, what's the worst that could happen?'

'Look, Aria,' said Grandma, equally attempting to make Aria understand, 'Firstly, it is important to understand the intentions your brother had. The vampires took Jayden for a reason. If your brother wouldn't have gone to the forest that day, then he would have gone to the forest on the next day. And even if you manage to distract him every time, the heavens know what he'd become—into a monster or still the same person. Travelling into the past is like dancing on a tightrope—one wrong step and the future may crumble.' warned Grandma.

'So, it's a no?' asked Aria. She perfectly understood Elleira, though was not giving up the bizarre idea.

Grandma gave a stiff look of disapproval. 'Though I must say, the idea was very well thought out.' remarked Grandma.

Aria gave a forced smile as dozens of thoughts came crashing into her head. It was as though her brother had not wanted Aria to find him. Tears streamed down through Aria's cheeks as she found all this overwhelming.

'Shh, it's alright,' consoled Grandma, as she approached Aria and embraced into a tight hug, 'I know you feel terrible for not knowing about this side of your brother, but he would have done it for a reason.'

'What do you mean?' asked Aria, confused.

Grandma slowly released Aria from the hug and said, 'He would have done it to protect you and everyone else. He wouldn't have wanted you to carry the burden. That's true sibling bond right there.'

Aria sniffed and wiped her tears and looked at Grandma Elleira, whose eyes were filled with tears of determination. Her brother had not told her about any of this, not even left a clue of the wizarding world before he was dragged away.

A clue... Aria pondered silently. If there was a thing, he would have given her before he was dragged away, then it would be something meaningful.

It was just then a brick of realisation fell over her head.

'The bracelet!' exclaimed Aria. Aria finally understood why Jayden had given it to her at the last moment.

'The what?' asked Grandma, who was oblivious to the storms that were brewing in Aria's head.

'The bracelet!' said Aria again, 'The one Jay gave me right before—'

'You're right!' gasped Elleira, 'Oh, why didn't I think of this before? The hint! Aria, your brother didn't leave you with nothing to find him. He wanted you to find him, and he is still waiting for it.'

Aria was amazed by the discovery she had made, after one whole month of having the clue with herself.

'I'm going to go home, and check for any clues he had left in the bracelet. Then, I'm going to bring it to you at the first light of dawn tomorrow, and we can check for any other clues or whether the bracelet is enchanted to hide the clue.'

'Of course, my dear,' said Grandma lovingly, 'Make sure that you check every nook of the bracelet, because the enchantment can be anywhere and everywhere.'

'Alright, Grandma, I guess I'd better get going.' said Aria, as she slung her bag over her shoulder.

'Wait, out of curiosity,' said Grandma, 'Why aren't you wearing the bracelet your brother gave to you?'

Aria expected this question to come out of Grandma's mouth. 'Whenever I wear the bracelet, it reminds me of that night, and only that night, Grandma. It just scares me to death, like what if my brother was a bad person and gave me this bracelet just as a mere token? Moreover, whenever I wear the bracelet, it's like the bracelet is trying to make me think that my brother was an evil person who did not share any of his secrets to his own sister. Wait,' said Aria, as she realised something, 'Grandma, do you think the bracelet has an enchantment of trying to make me think the opposite of who they are?'

Grandma shook her head and smiled warmly. 'Aria, not everything is made from spells and enchantments. Most of them are made up of our memories, character and even mystery.'

Aria nodded in understanding and opened the back door, 'Well, Grandma, will see you tomorrow.'

'Take care, sweetie. Good night!' said Grandma.

'Good night!' yelled back Aria as she closed the door and set off on the lane.

It was a chilly evening and to the left of the lane, Aria saw lots of vehicles passing by on the Saturday evening.

As Aria reached home, she saw her aunt cooking dinner. She hadn't spoken to her mother since morning and wanted to talk to her. Her uncle, Harold, was out for work, as usual.

'Hi, Mrs. Miller.' Aria said as she locked the door behind her. Her aunt barely acknowledged her, turning only to glance at Aria before resuming her work.

'Hi,' Jesse replied curtly, her tone devoid of warmth. 'How was your day?'

'It was fine. We found a lot of interesting things.' Aria said, trying to sound enthusiastic but sensing her aunt's lack of interest.

'Good for you. Are you ready for dinner now?' Jesse asked, her arms crossed tightly.

'I'll freshen up and be back in a minute.' Aria replied, feeling the pressure of her aunt's scrutinising gaze.

She walked to her bedroom, grabbed a set of pyjamas, took a quick bath, and changed out of her clothes. The loose-fitting pants and shirt offered some relief from the stifling humidity.

Aria sat at the dining table, staring down at the vegetable frittata her Aunt Jesse had prepared. The dish—once her favourite—now tasted bland, just like everything else in her life since Jayden had disappeared, and her parents were gone. She forced herself to take a bite, the food sitting heavy in her mouth, each chew reminding her of how different everything had become.

She remembered how lively dinner used to be. Every evening, the four of them—Aria, Jayden, and their parents—would gather around the same table, their laughter filling the room, sharing stories about their day. Her father always had some funny anecdotes from work, and her mother would tease them both with her playful wit. Jayden, ever the joker, would try to imitate their father, exaggerating his expressions just to make everyone laugh.

It was a warmth she could feel even now, an unspoken bond between them, made stronger with every shared meal.

But now, those days were gone.

The once comforting buzz of conversation had been replaced by an uncomfortable silence. No Jayden, no parents. Just her, under the cold, penetrating glare of Aunt Jesse. Every night felt like a chore.

Aria would sit across from her aunt, both wordlessly picking at their food. Jesse wasn't unkind, but she wasn't warm either—just distant, strict, and always so sharp with her words. There were no jokes, no stories, no laughter, just the clink of cutlery on plates and Jesse's occasional disapproving comments.

'Eat up. Don't waste time.' Jesse ordered, her voice slicing through the quiet, more out of duty than care. Aria nodded, trying to swallow the lump in her throat along with the bite of food.

'Thanks, Mrs. Miller.' Aria said quietly, her voice barely above a whisper, as if speaking too loudly would shatter the thin peace between them. She didn't expect a warm reply—Jesse never really paid much attention to Aria's emotions. She was too caught up in her own world of rigid rules.

'Don't mention it.' Jesse replied without even glancing up, her attention focused solely on her meal. The words were mechanical, devoid of any warmth or connection, leaving Aria feeling even more alone.

Aria's eyes drifted to the empty chairs around the table, their absence echoing louder than any sound in the room. She could almost picture her parents there—her mother handing her father a napkin, Jayden grinning as he reached for another helping of dessert.

It felt so close, so real, like she could just reach out and touch them. But it was only an illusion, a memory that faded away the moment she blinked.

The silence that stretched between her and Aunt Jesse was suffocating, the house too quiet, too still. Aria missed the noise, the mess, the love that had once filled these walls. Now it was just her, alone with her thoughts and memories that never quite left her in peace.

She finished her meal in silence, her mind drifting far away from the cold dining room. The food that once brought comfort now served as a reminder of all she had lost. As she pushed her plate aside and excused herself, Aria couldn't help but wonder if there would ever be a time when the house would feel alive again, or if it would always feel like this—empty, cold, and full of ghosts.

Aria washed her plate. 'I'm going to my room to do some assignments, Mrs. Miller.' she mumbled, her heart sinking as she crossed the dining room, acutely aware of her aunt's indifference.

'Fine. Just keep the noise down.' Jesse replied without looking up, leaving Aria to feel more alone than ever as she retreated to her room.

As she stepped inside, the familiar scent of her room enveloped her, bringing a sense of comfort and nostalgia.

She walked over to her desk. Opening the top drawer, Aria's fingers brushed against a beautifully carved wooden box. It was a cherished possession, holding memories that were precious to her.

With a soft click, she opened the box, revealing a collection of items that Jayden had given her over the years. Each piece held a story, a memory shared between them. Among the treasures, one item caught her attention—the delicate orange bracelet with a silver half-pendant.

Aria picked up the bracelet and sat on her bed, her fingers tracing the intricate patterns on the pendant. She could almost see Jayden, sitting with intense focus, his small hands carefully working the threads, his tongue probably poking out in concentration as he meticulously crafted the bracelet.

At first glance, nothing seemed unusual—all she saw was hard work, effort and love in making the detailed bracelet. She admired the skill, thinking of the time and effort he must have put into making it just for her.

But as she was about to set it aside, something unusual caught her eye. She noticed a small slit in the pendant. It wasn't part of the original design; it looked like Jayden had made it himself.

Driven by the need to uncover whatever secret her brother might have hidden; Aria grabbed a needle from her desk. Aria grabbed a needle and carefully poked into the opening.

Suddenly, a soft rustle reached her ears—the unmistakable sound of paper. Gently, she pulled out a tiny scroll, no bigger than a fingertip.

Unrolling the minuscule note, Aria squinted at the writing, but it was too small to read.

Frustrated, she remembered the microscope her biology teacher, Miss Loomy, had handed out a few weeks ago as a reward for their class's hard work. She had barely touched it since, but now, it seemed like it might be her only hope.

She took the microscope from her desk and placed the tiny note under the lens. Adjusting the focus, she peered through, but even with the magnification, the writing was still too small to read clearly. Disappointed, Aria realised she'd have to wait until morning to ask Grandma

Elleira for help. Perhaps there was a magical spell that could enlarge the words.

As she sat back, holding the bracelet in her hand, something clicked in her mind. How had Jayden managed to write something so impossibly small? It seemed like no ordinary task—it was as if he had gone to great lengths to conceal whatever message he had left for her.

Just then, the pieces of the puzzle began to fall into place. Aria's eyes widened in realisation. Jayden hadn't just written the note with an ordinary pen.

He must have used magic. It was the only explanation.

Her brother, always so clever and full of surprises, had found a way to hide a secret message in the one place he knew she would eventually find it.

As Aria clutched the bracelet in her hand, an overwhelming wave of emotions washed over her. Love for her brother, who had always been her anchor, surged through her heart. But alongside that love was a deep curiosity, a burning desire to understand the hidden message Jayden had left behind.

What secrets could this small piece of jewellery hold? What was her brother trying to tell her?

With each passing moment, her sense of determination grew stronger. This wasn't just a trinket—it was a key. A key to unlocking something far bigger, something that could lead her to Jayden. She didn't know where the path would take her, but one thing was clear: she wouldn't stop until she uncovered the truth.

No matter what challenges lay ahead, she was ready to face them, because this was about more than just finding answers—it was about finding him.

And she was going to do whatever it took to uncover it.

CHAPTER TEN

Beneath the Moonlight

When the first rays of dawn appeared, Aria found herself walking through the familiar route to Grandma Elleira's shop. She wondered how long her brother had known about the supernatural world.

What made him know about magic in the first place—was it intentional or a coincidence?

She reached the shop, but did not see Grandma at the front counter. Then, she went round the shop and opened the back door. There, she saw Elleira, who turned her head, and was supposedly reading a book, which looked like the Grimoire.

'Hi, Aria. I didn't see you there.' greeted Grandma, pulling a chair from the back for Aria.

'Hi, Grandma. What are you looking at?' asked Aria, her eyes fixed on the book as she closed the door behind her.

'Oh, just the Grimoire, dear. I've been flipping through its pages quite a lot recently.' Grandma chuckled.

'Hmm,' Aria responded absent-mindedly before shifting her tone. 'Well, you were right again.'

'What do you mean?' asked Grandma, her attention now fully on Aria as she shifted her focus away from Grimoire.

'I checked his room yesterday after I got home, and—' Aria paused, untying the half-pendant bracelet from her wrist, '—I found this.'

She handed the bracelet over to Grandma Elleira. Elleira gently turned the bracelet over in her fingers, examining it closely.

'This is intriguing,' said Grandma, admiring the braided orange bracelet. 'I can sense some magic in it. Supernatural magic.'

'Yes, I think so too,' Aria agreed. 'I found a note hidden in a hand-made slit in the pendant, but the writing was so small I couldn't read it, even under a microscope.'

'Wait. Let me look.' said Elleira. She followed the same steps Aria had taken the night before, retrieving the note from the pendant. She unfolded it and began to read.

Aria's eyes widened in surprise. *How is she able to read it?* she wondered.

'Grandma, how can you read the note?' Aria asked, voicing the question buzzing in her mind.

Grandma Elleira smiled knowingly, as though the answer was second nature to her. 'Oh, my dear, all supernatural beings possess exceptional eyesight. It doesn't matter how tiny the writing is or how well-hidden something might be—we can always see it clearly.'

'So, does that mean vampires, too, have such keen eyesight?' asked Aria.

'Yes, all supernatural beings do, including me.' Grandma confirmed.

Aria nodded, absorbing the information, before turning her focus back to the note in Grandma's hands. 'Anyway, what does it say?'

'Do you want me to read it aloud?' Grandma asked gently, her eyes soft but curious.

'Yes, please.' Aria replied, her voice steady but filled with anticipation.

Grandma's voice became soft but clear, as though she understood the weight the words carried for Aria. 'Sissy, I'm sorry that I'm leaving you. I know it's going to be hard for you, but it's the only way right now. I don't know where I will be in that world, but I know you can find me. I'm waiting for you.'

'He added a P.S. note too—Follow the stars when the moon is full and look for the tree that never sleeps. It holds the door to where our worlds meet.'

Aria sat still, her hands trembling as she heard Grandma read the note. Her brother's words echoed in her mind, filling her with a mixture of hope and confusion.

The message was cryptic, yet it carried an undeniable weight. She had always suspected there was more to Jayden's disappearance, but now... now she had proof.

'Wait for a full moon... follow the stars to the tree that never sleeps.' she whispered aloud. What tree? Where? Her mind raced with possibilities. It couldn't just be an ordinary tree—it had to be something magical, something hidden from the everyday world.

Her heart pounded as the realisation set in: Jayden was alive. Somewhere. He had left her this clue, knowing she would find it, knowing she would come after him. And now, after a month of feeling lost without him, she had a path—no matter how uncertain—towards finding him again.

Grandma Elleira must have sensed the shift in Aria's emotions, for she stepped closer and gently wrapped her arms around her granddaughter. 'Your brother,' she whispered in Aria's ear, 'is one of the cleverest boys of his age.'

'I know,' said Aria with pride. 'I just wish it hadn't taken me so long to see the truth. One whole month—'

'Shh,' Grandma interrupted softly, sensing Aria's guilt. 'It's not your fault, Aria—It's the vampires'. Your brother had a plan, more than just leaving you behind with questions. He was protecting you.'

Aria nodded, trying to gather her thoughts and calm the storm inside her. 'Right,' she said, straightening her posture. 'But Grandma, do you know anything about the tree that was mentioned in the note?'

Grandma paused for a moment, thinking deeply. 'Hmm, we did not walk through trees when we were in battles. I haven't seen the vampire world yet—we've only met on the battlefield. All I know is that their world is vast. Bigger than ours, as they are enormous in numbers. However, was there ever a special tree, one that was significant to both of you?' she asked, her brow slightly raised as she searched Aria's face for any recognition.

Aria furrowed her brow in thought. 'Not that I remember of,' she replied slowly. She tried to think of all the places she and Jayden had played, but nothing stood out. They had never had a specific tree that was important to them—at least, not that she could recall. It was always just random trees near the school or parks. Jayden wouldn't have hidden a note *there*.

'Well then,' Grandma said with a gentle smile, 'I suppose we'll just have to figure it out together, won't we?'

Aria smiled faintly, a mixture of determination and anxiety bubbling inside her. She nodded. 'Yes,' she whispered, 'We will.'

Grandma handed the note back to Aria. She clutched the tiny note close to her chest, her breath shaky but her resolve steady. 'I'm coming, Jayden,' she whispered, her voice determined. 'I'll find you, wherever you are.'

She reached out to pat Aria's hand gently, her touch soft but full of strength. 'You've always had a fire in you, Aria. It's what will guide you through even the darkest of paths. Don't lose that determination, no matter what lies ahead.'

Aria felt a swell of reassurance from Elleira's words, the weight of the situation lightened just a little.

Aria felt a mix of emotions welling up inside her—determination, hope, and a strong sense of purpose. Holding the tiny note in her hand, she realised that this wasn't just a small message from her brother; it was the start of something much bigger. It was a challenge, an invitation to step into a world she had only heard about in stories. The thought of finding Jayden and bringing him back filled her with resolve, and she knew she couldn't turn back now.

But deep down, Aria also knew that this journey wouldn't be easy. The magical world her brother had hinted at wasn't just some fantasy; it was real, and it was dangerous. The world she knew—full of ordinary things and everyday people—was just a small part of a much larger, more complex reality.

There would be risks, challenges, and dangers she couldn't even begin to imagine. She would have to be brave, smart, and ready for anything that came her way.

Aria took a deep breath and looked up at Grandma Elleira, who was watching her with a mix of pride and concern. 'I'm ready, Grandma,' she said, her voice steady. 'I'm going to find Jayden and bring him back, no matter what it takes.'

Grandma Elleira gave her a warm smile, but her eyes were serious. 'And I'll be here to help you every step of the way, my dear. But you must understand, this journey will test you in ways you've never been tested before. You'll need to stay strong, trust your instincts, and keep your heart in the right place. There will be times when things get tough, but you must never give up.'

Aria nodded, feeling the weight of Elleira's words. She knew this was going to be difficult, but with Grandma by her side and the thought of finding Jayden guiding her, she felt ready to face whatever lay ahead. She had a long road in front of her, filled with unknowns, but she was determined to see it through.

As she stood there, she could almost hear Jayden's voice in her mind, urging her forward, telling her that he believed in her. And with that, Aria knew that no matter what dangers or challenges came her way, she wouldn't stop until she found her brother and brought him back home.

Aria took a deep breath, steadying herself as she felt the enormity of the task ahead. She carefully folded the tiny note, slipping it back into the slit in the pendant. The weight of the bracelet in her hand was a reminder of Jayden's message. She didn't care that it was going to make her remember about the dreadful moment at the forest—all she wanted was her brother's presence in her.

'Grandma,' she began, her voice soft but resolute, 'Where do we start? How do we find this tree that never sleeps?'

Elleira's eyes twinkled with a mixture of wisdom and mystery. 'The journey to find the tree will require more than just knowledge, Aria. It will require heart, intuition, and a connection to the world beyond the ordinary. The tree that never sleeps is not just a place; it's a gateway, hidden from those who are not meant to find it. But I believe you are meant to find it, just as your brother was.'

Aria listened intently, absorbing Elleira's words. 'How do we begin?' she asked again, this time with a stronger sense of determination.

'We begin with preparation,' Grandma replied. 'We'll need to gather supplies, but more importantly, you'll need to strengthen your understanding of the magical world.'

'Magic,' Aria whispered, the word feeling both foreign and familiar on her tongue. 'But I don't know any magic, Grandma. How can I possibly do this?'

Elleira placed a reassuring hand on Aria's shoulder. 'Magic is not just about spells and incantations. It's about belief, about the energy you put into the world, and the connections you make with it. You've always had a spark of magic within you, Aria, even if you haven't realised it yet. This journey will help you awaken it.'

Aria felt a rush of warmth and confidence from Grandma's words. She had always felt a deep connection to nature, to the stars, and to the world around her, but she had never thought of it as something magical.

Now, it all started to make sense—the little things she noticed, the feelings she had when she was alone in the woods, or under the night sky. It was as if the world had been speaking to her all along, and she was finally beginning to understand its language.

'We'll start by finding more about the vampire world—to have a clear view on the battlefield,' Grandma Elleira continued. 'And while we're at it, we'll also seek out any clues about the tree. It may be mentioned in the Grimoire.'

Aria nodded, her mind racing with thoughts and possibilities. 'And what about the full moon? Jay mentioned about following the stars when the moon is full. Shouldn't we wait until then?'

'Yes,' said Grandma. 'As I've told you before, the full moon holds special power, and it will reveal things that are hidden during other times. But we don't have to wait idly. There's much to do in the meantime to prepare. When the night of the full moon comes, we'll be ready to embark on the journey.'

'So, where do we start?' asked Aria.

'We've already started,' replied Elleira with a reassuring smile. 'Now, we just need to see it through and get your brother back. First, we'll go through the Grimoire, look for any spells that could help us, and figure out the rest as we go.'

'Ok, but what kind of spells?' asked Aria tentatively.

'Everything connected to this moment,' replied Grandma. 'Though, I've been thinking about meeting the coven tonight. Would you like to come along?'

'Sure, but why?' asked Aria, puzzled.

'Well, we're not entirely sure how to proceed, are we?' said Grandma thoughtfully. 'I figured meeting the coven might be our best bet. They could help us sift through the Grimoire and possibly uncover any useful spells. Who knows? We might even figure this whole thing out tonight.'

'Alright, then. So tonight, we head to the Enchanted Summit.' Aria declared.

Grandma gave a firm nod as she began packing the essentials. She reached for her old-fashioned backpack, carefully stuffing the Grimoire into the large compartment. She gathered her water bottle, a few muffins, and zipped it up. Glancing out the window, she noticed the fading light. Twilight had already set in.

'Don't you think it's time we leave?' asked Grandma Elleira.

'Yeah, I suppose we should.' Aria agreed.

'Good,' said Grandma. 'But Aria, keep in mind—it's a full moon tonight. Vampires might be out roaming, so we must stay cautious.'

'Got it.' said Aria. She was ready to venture tonight, but the thought of vampires gave her chills down the spine.

She couldn't shake the images of pale faces lurking in the shadows, their eyes glowing like embers. What if one of them crossed their path? Her heart raced at the mere thought, but she knew she had to stay strong for Grandma's sake.

The excitement of the adventure clashed with the dread of the unknown, leaving her feeling both exhilarated and terrified.

As Aria and Grandma walked through the once familiar path, a familiar sensation of eeriness and anticipation filled the air.

'Lumière.' said Grandma, in a clear voice, as she flicked her wand. A bright, golden light emanated from the tip of the ebony-coloured wand, illuminating the surroundings. The sudden brightness startled the nocturnal creatures hiding in the shadows, their glowing eyes momentarily reflecting the light before they vanished into the darkness.

The woods were dark and dense, with shadows stretching out like skeletal hands in the flickering light. The trees loomed high, their branches swaying gently as if whispering secrets to one another. The path ahead seemed to narrow and twist, making Aria wonder if they were even going in the right direction.

'Stay close, Aria,' Grandma whispered. 'This forest can play tricks on your mind, especially at night.'

Aria tightened her grip on the small dagger hidden in her cloak. It wasn't much, but it made her feel slightly more secure. As they continued, the sounds of nocturnal creatures rustled around them. Occasionally, Aria caught glimpses of glowing eyes in the underbrush, vanishing the moment the light of Grandma's wand came near.

After what felt like hours of walking, they reached a small clearing where the ground was covered in a soft, silver mist. In the centre stood the ancient tree—the one marked with the crescent moon cradled in vines.

'There it is,' Aria breathed, her voice barely a whisper. The tree towered above them, its bark gnarled and twisted, glistening with a faint, eerie light. Symbols were carved deep into its trunk, glowing softly as if in response to their presence.

Grandma approached cautiously, her eyes scanning the intricate markings. 'This is no ordinary tree,' she murmured. 'It's an ancient doorway, a living boundary between our world and theirs.'

Aria felt a shiver run down her spine as she watched Grandma trace her fingers over one of the symbols. 'What now?' she asked, her voice trembling slightly.

'Now,' replied Grandma, her voice steady and comforting amidst the chilling silence of the woods, 'As we discussed earlier, we need not venture into their world just yet. We've done well to locate the tree; it will be easier to find when the time comes. For now, let's move forward. We came here for another purpose tonight—to find our coven.'

The way Grandma said 'our coven' sent a warm glow through Aria's heart. Although she had no supernatural powers of her own, hearing Grandma include her so naturally made her feel deeply connected to this mystical world.

There was something reassuring about being part of something so ancient and profound. The sense of belonging washed over her like a wave, banishing her earlier doubts.

Grandma's words filled Aria with newfound courage. If Elleira could include her as part of this coven, then maybe she was more capable than she had ever imagined. She took a deep breath and nodded, the cold air filling her lungs as she embraced the thrill of the unknown.

'Let's go,' Aria said, her voice carrying an edge of determination. She was ready to face whatever lay ahead, knowing that this was just the beginning of her connection to a world brimming with magic and mystery.

The trees around them grew denser, their branches intertwining above like a twisted canopy, blocking out the moonlight. The air was filled with the scent of damp earth and moss, and each step they took was accompanied by the soft crunch of leaves underfoot. The only light came from the glowing tip of Grandma's wand, casting eerie shadows that danced around them.

As they walked, Grandma kept a keen eye on their surroundings, her movements purposeful. 'We're getting closer,' she whispered, glancing around as though expecting something to appear, with the light of the wand guiding the way. 'The coven is hidden, shielded by magic. Only those who know where to look can find it.'

Aria swallowed, feeling a knot of anticipation tighten in her stomach. Finding the coven was crucial; they needed the wizards' wisdom to safely enter the vampire realm and rescue her brother, Jayden.

As they moved forward, the path became less discernible, merging into a tangle of overgrown roots and shrubs. Aria's heart raced with each step. She knew they were venturing into territory that few dared to tread, and the thrill of it both scared and excited her.

'We don't need the light anymore,' said Grandma, as she flicked her wand. 'Obscurité,' said Elleira, and the light became dim, then went off.

As the minutes turned into hours, the forest around them remained eerily quiet. Just when Aria began to wonder if they were in the right place, she saw movement at the edge of the clearing. Her heart skipped a beat as robed figures began to emerge from the shadows, their faces illuminated by the moonlight.

A woman stepped forward and lowered her hood. It was Alice, the same woman they had met weeks ago. Her expression softened into a smile as she recognized Grandma.

'Arielle,' she greeted warmly, her voice carrying a note of familiarity. 'Back so soon? We had a feeling you might return.'

Grandma returned the smile, her eyes gleaming with the comfort of reunion. 'Alice,' she said, stepping forward. 'We knew we'd need to see you again. There's still much we need to discuss.'

Alice's gaze shifted to Aria, her expression both curious and welcoming. 'And young Aria,' she acknowledged with a nod. 'It's good to see you've joined us once more.'

Aria nodded back, feeling a mix of anticipation and relief. Though she had met this coven only once before, the connection Elleira shared with them made the encounter feel strangely comforting.

Without hesitation, Grandma moved toward Alice, enveloping her in a warm hug. This time, it was not the cautious embrace of strangers but that of old friends rekindling their bond.

One by one, the other cloaked figures lowered their hoods, revealing familiar faces—each of them greeting Grandma with a mixture of smiles and nods (Aria recognized Persephone, Phineas Gabrielle and Reginald by his stiff posture).

Alice placed a gentle hand on Grandma's arm. 'We know why you're here,' she said quietly, her voice tinged with understanding. 'Come, let's continue where we left off. There is much to discuss and even more to prepare for.'

'Yes,' said Reginald, his deep voice echoing through the circle. 'If you intend to enter the vampire world, you must be prepared for what you will face. This is not just a matter of finding the tree; it's about crossing into an entirely different realm.'

Phineas stepped forward, his expression both serious and curious. 'So, you found the tree?' asked Phineas. Grandma and Aria nodded. 'We did, with the help of Jayden's note.' said Aria.

'That's impressive. Not many can locate the portal, let alone survive the magic guarding it.' His eyes flicked to Aria with a mix of respect and challenge. 'You must have more courage than most.'

Aria flushed at the compliment, feeling a mix of pride and fear. 'We found it,' said Aria again, her voice steady. 'But we need your help to cross over safely and bring my brother back.'

Persephone, who had been silent until now, stepped forward and placed a gentle hand on Aria's shoulder. 'Crossing into the vampire realm is not just about magic,' she said softly. 'It's about understanding the balance of power. The vampires will test you, mentally and emotionally. Our magic can protect you, but it can't shield you from the trials you'll face there.'

Grandma nodded, her eyes scanning each member of the coven. 'We know the risks. That's why we've come to you. We need spells, protection, and guidance to prepare ourselves.'

Persephone exchanged a glance with the others before speaking. 'There are ancient spells in the Grimoire that can aid you,' she said, 'But, haven't you gone through it already?'

'Yes, Persephone, but we were not able to figure out the right spell or potion for finding Jayden. That's one of the many reasons why we came to see you all.' said Elleira.

'Well, of course there'd be the right spells and potions,' said the witch named Gabrielle, 'We'll search for it together. But the price of using these spells is high. They require energy, focus, and above all, sacrifice.'

'Not just physical sacrifices, either,' Reginald interjected, his gaze locking onto Grandma. 'Emotional sacrifices. The spell requires you to confront your deepest fears and regrets. It will dig into your memories and use them as a key to open the portal.'

'The one like the Memory Retrieval Charm,' said Grandma softly to Aria.

Aria's eyes widened. 'So... You might have to relive some of your worst memories to enter their world?'

Phineas nodded grimly. 'Exactly; more like reliving truths. That's how they keep intruders out. The vampire realm feeds on emotional agitation. You must face it head-on if you hope to succeed.'

Alice's voice was calm and reassuring as she added, 'But don't be afraid, Aria. You're not alone in this. We'll teach you how to strengthen your mind and guard your heart.'

Persephone flipped through the pages of the Grimoire, searching for the right spell. 'Well, it's not here. Who would've thought to include a spell to enter the vampire world?' She sighed. 'Looks like we'll have to create one ourselves. Alright, everyone, gather around.'

The coven quickly formed a circle, raising their wands in unison. Aria watched in awe as a blue streak of light shot out from each wand, swirling around them like a ribbon of energy. The lights intertwined, connecting with each other, forming a glowing web of magic.

The wizards began to chant an unfamiliar incantation, their voices harmonising as the swirling light gradually changed into detailed intricate symbols, radiating a powerful sense of unity.

As the ritual neared its end, a ripple of excitement spread through the group. The light slowly faded, leaving behind the newly formed symbols etched in the air. A murmur ran through the circle.

'Aria! Come here.' called Persephone. Aria pushed through the circle to join her.

'Here it is.' Persephone said, pointing to the intricate symbols now glowing faintly on a page that had appeared in the Grimoire. 'The Spell of Passage. It's complex and requires all of us to cast it together.'

'You all created this just now, in a matter of seconds?' Aria asked, her eyes wide as she gazed at the delicate patterns on the worn page.

Persephone and Grandma Elleira exchanged a quick glance and nodded. 'Yes,' Persephone replied. 'Magic is a force of will and unity, especially when a coven comes together with a shared purpose.'

'What exactly do we need for this spell?' Aria asked, a hint of nervousness in her voice.

The wizard named Gabrielle sighed, as though explaining this part would not be easy. 'The Spell of Passage requires more than just ingredients. It demands bravery. Here's how it works: First, we'll need the Grimoire itself, this very book.' She pointed to the ancient tome.

'Next, there's a special serum—Truth Serum—that forces you to confront your deepest memories, both joyful and painful. Then, we must create a magical circle on the ground, marked with symbols of protection, to act as the gateway between worlds.'

Phineas, another member of the coven, stepped forward with a mysterious smile. 'The riddle inscribed in the Grimoire might explain it better. Look,' he said.

Aria and the coven gathered around the ancient Grimoire that Phineas was holding to look at the riddle. Silence settled over the yard; everyone's attention drawn to the words that had the power to unlock the vampire world.

To journey beyond and open the way,
Through truths hidden deep, you must not stray.
First, take the tome where secrets lie,
Its ink of old marks where worlds collide.

A draught of truth you must partake,
Face memories past, for the path to wake.
Draw the circle, symbols clear,
Protection against what you hold dear.

Not alone can this be done,
A circle of power, many as one.
Speak the words, ancient and wise,
To find the passage where mystery lies.

Name each piece you'll need for the night
For the key to the gate, to worlds out of sight.

Phineas closed the Grimoire, the air around them thick with anticipation. 'The riddle hints at the components: the Grimoire, that is the tome itself, the Truth Serum, the protective circle, and the power of the coven working as one.'

Aria swallowed hard, absorbing the information. 'So, if we do all this, the passage to the vampire world will open?'

'Yes,' replied Grandma, her eyes steady. 'But remember, the path is treacherous. We must confront our fears and face the truths of our past, for the passage feeds on emotions left unresolved.'

With that understanding, Aria felt a mix of fear and determination. They were one step closer to finding her brother, but the road ahead would be anything but easy.

Grandma looked at each member of the coven, her face a mix of determination and gratitude. 'Thank you,' she said earnestly. 'We're ready to do whatever it takes.'

Persephone nodded, her expression softening. 'We'll start with basic protective charms and wards. Over the next few days, you'll need to focus on meditation. The stronger your mind, the better chance you'll have against the illusions of the vampire world.'

Reginald stepped forward, raising his hands as swirling lights appeared between his palms. 'I'll teach you the shielding spell. It's crucial for protecting your thoughts. The vampires are skilled at reading emotions. This spell will help you to control your thoughts and protect your mind.'

'Wait, so vampires can read thoughts too?' Aria asked, her surprise growing with every new revelation.

'Not exactly,' replied Alice. 'But they do get a rough sense of what we're thinking.'

'Isn't that just like what normal humans can do?' Aria questioned.

'A bit different,' Alice continued, choosing her words carefully. 'Humans might get a sense of what someone else is feeling—a gut instinct, a subtle clue. But vampires, they go deeper. They can sense the intentions behind your thoughts, almost like a whisper they can't quite hear but can feel. It's not the exact words in your head, but more like the pulse of your emotions and desires.'

Aria's eyes widened. 'So, they can sense if we're lying or hiding something?'

'Precisely,' Alice nodded. 'That's why when we face them, we must guard our emotions. Keep your mind focused and clear, or they might pick up on your fears and doubts. Vampires are skilled at exploiting weaknesses, so even a stray thought can become a weapon in their hands.'

Gabrielle placed a vial of clear liquid into Grandma's hand. 'This is a truth serum,' she explained. 'But not to use on others—on yourself. When you drink it, you'll confront your deepest fears. You must drink it before entering their world. Only by facing your own truth can you pass through the tree.'

Grandma felt a shiver of fear run through her at Gabrielle's words, but she swallowed and nodded. 'I'll do it,' she said resolutely. 'For Jayden.'

'We now have about a month or three days to prepare, before the next full moon,' said Alice, 'During that time, we will teach and train you. When the time comes, we will cast the spell together to open the way.'

Grandma squeezed Aria's hand. 'We'll be ready,' she said, her voice filled with determination.

'Then it's settled,' Alice said, giving a small, approving nod. 'We'll meet again in about three days. But of course, you are welcome to come here anytime, Arielle.'

'Until then, keep your hearts focused and your minds sharp. The vampire world is no place for hesitation.' said Reginald seriously.

The coven members slowly retreated into the shadows, their forms fading into the mist.

Aria stood still for a moment, absorbing the enormity of what lay ahead. She turned to Grandma, who gave her a reassuring smile. 'Let's go, dear,' Grandma said softly. 'We have so much to do.'

They walked back through the forest, the path now seeming darker, more mysterious. Aria's mind whirled with everything they had learned and the preparations they needed to make. The truth serum, protection circle, the portal—everything was swirling in her head.

As they approached the tree, they felt the air grow cold and still. Grandma turned to Aria; her eyes filled with steely resolve. 'Remember what we've learned,' she whispered. 'Stay focused, and we'll find him.'

She felt the weight of the journey ahead but also a glimmer of hope, knowing they had the coven's support. The journey back was filled with a quiet determination.

By the time Aria reached home, exhaustion had crept in. Aria changed into her pyjamas and slipped into bed, her mind racing with all that had happened.

The next morning, she woke early and headed to school, feeling a strange mixture of excitement and nerves. She moved through the day, attending classes, exchanging greetings with her friends, and listening to the teachers' lectures, though her mind was elsewhere.

After school, Aria made her way to Elleira's shop. Grandma was already there, flipping through the Grimoire. 'Ah, there you are,' she greeted as Aria entered. 'I've found something new.'

Aria's heart skipped a beat as she approached the counter where Grandma Elleira sat, the ancient Grimoire spread wide open, its yellowed pages glowing softly in the dim light of the shop. 'What did you find?' Aria asked, curiosity bubbling within her as she leaned over to get a better look.

Grandma pointed to a page filled with symbols and text written in a language Aria couldn't fully understand.

'This,' said Grandma, tapping the page gently, 'is a forgotten spell.'

The Spell of Shared Sight

Incantation: Visus Coniunge

To see the world through another's gaze,
Bring forth an object from their days.
A lock, a trinket, something dear,
The bond between must be clear.

Though eyes align and visions share,
Move not, or you'll break the pair.

If too long you stay, your mind may sway,
With heads that ache and thoughts astray.

'The Spell of Shared Sight?' Aria asked doubtfully. It sounded intriguing, but what was the purpose behind it?

'It's an ancient connection spell, one that could help us establish a direct link to the vampire world.' Grandma explained.

'But how would that be helpful?' Aria questioned.

'We can use this spell to see what your brother sees.' Grandma replied.

Aria's eyes widened. 'So, we could actually experience what he's going through?'

'Yes,' Grandma said, her tone serious. 'It's our best chance to understand his situation and find a way to rescue him. We'll be able to see his surroundings and the vampires he's with.'

Aria felt a rush of hope mixed with apprehension. 'But what if it's dangerous? What if we see something we're not supposed to?'

Grandma placed a reassuring hand on her shoulder. 'We'll be cautious. The spell allows us to view without being seen ourselves. We'll remain hidden in the shadows of his vision.'

'Okay,' Aria said, taking a deep breath. 'Let's do it. I need to help him.'

'Then we need to gather the components for the spell,' Grandma replied, her voice steady, 'We'll need a personal item of Jayden's to create the link. It should be something that carries his energy.'

'Like his favourite cap?' Aria suggested.

'Yes, that would work. Let's find it and prepare for the spell tonight.' Grandma said, determination in her eyes.

As they began to plan, Aria felt a surge of courage. This was her chance to connect with Jayden, to see what he was facing, and perhaps even to bring him back.

CHAPTER ELEVEN

The Path Ahead

Aria stood in front of the Grimoire, her fingers tracing the ancient symbols on the page. Grandma had prepared everything: candles flickered in a perfect circle around her, and the air was thick with the scent of sage.

'Ready?' Grandma asked, her voice calm but serious.

Aria nodded, 'I'll be careful,' she promised, though her heart felt heavy with the unknown.

She had never attempted anything like this before—joining her vision with Jayden's, seeing the world through his eyes. But they needed answers, and this was the only way to find out what the vampires were planning while keeping Jayden safely within the shop.

'Take a deep breath, focus on the bond.' Grandma instructed.

Closing her eyes, Grandma spoke the incantation aloud, the ancient words rolling off her tongue with a strange familiarity.

'Visus Coniunge.' said Grandma, in a clear voice.

The spell hummed through the air, invisible but tangible, as if the very fabric of reality was shifting around them.

Aria gasped as the world tilted. Her vision blurred, then sharpened—only it wasn't the sanctuary she was seeing anymore. It was the forest. Dark trees stretched high into the sky, and the ground beneath 'her' feet was damp with fallen leaves. She could feel Jayden's heartbeat, quick and steady, his breath shallow as he crept forward cautiously.

She was seeing through Jayden's eyes.

'Jayden?' she whispered, though she knew he couldn't hear her. His mind was sharp and focused on his task.

In the distance, she caught sight of something—movement between the trees. Three figures, cloaked in shadows, glided through the forest. Aria felt the hairs on the back of her neck rise as she realised who they were. Vampires.

They moved silently, their glowing red eyes scanning the forest. Jayden's vision narrowed in on them, his body crouching low as he hid behind a large boulder. Aria could feel his tension, his wariness. He was dangerously close to them, close enough to overhear.

'It's almost time,' one of the vampires murmured, his voice a low hiss. 'Once the blood moon is fully risen, we'll draw the power. The relic will be ready, and the gateway will open.'

'Are the preparations complete?' another asked, her voice sharp and commanding.

'Yes,' replied the first. 'The human boy's research has proven useful. He'll lead us straight to the relic's resting place without even realising it.'

Aria's heart raced as the realisation hit her. Jayden had been a pawn in their game. They had used him to find the relic, and now they were going to activate it.

She felt Jayden tense, the realisation dawning on him at the same moment. Jayden's breath hitched as he slowly began to retreat, trying not to draw attention.

But it was too late.

One of the vampires' heads snapped in his direction, red eyes glowing ominously. 'Not so fast.'

Jayden's body froze, fear crashing over him. Aria's own heart thundered in her chest as she experienced his terror.

'Run, Jayden!' she whispered frantically, though she knew that her voice would reach no one.

She could feel his panic, the sudden burst of adrenaline as his feet moved on instinct, dashing through the trees. Branches whipped against his face; the sound of rushing wind filled his ears as he darted away from the vampires.

But they were faster. Shadows blurred beside him, and suddenly, a figure loomed in his path, blocking his escape. A vampire stepped forward, its fangs gleaming in the dim light.

Aria could feel Jayden's breath catch, his hand reaching for the dagger hidden beneath his jacket. But it was no use. They were too strong, too close.

As the vampire lunged toward him, everything went dark.

With a gasp, Aria snapped back into her own body, collapsing onto the floor of the shop. Her chest heaved as she struggled to catch her breath, her heart racing as if she had been the one running for her life.

'Aria!' Grandma was by her side in an instant, her hands on Aria's shoulders. 'We have to go!'

'Jayden...' Aria panted, her eyes wide with fear. 'He's in trouble. The vampires... they know. They're using him to find the relic!'

'I know, I also saw through his eyes,' Grandma's expression darkened. 'We need to act quickly.'

'Wait, you were with me the whole time?' Aria asked, still trying to wrap her head around it. Grandma nodded, a small smile. 'Of course.'

Aria wiped the sweat from her brow, still feeling Jayden's panic. 'We need to get to him before they do. Before it's too late.'

'We have to get the coven's help,' said Grandma Elleira, tapping her staff thrice against the ground. The green gem at its tip flickered momentarily before turning a vivid red, signalling urgency.

'We're on the move. Meet us at the vampire portal, which is right before a large, withered tree.' said Grandma, as though she was speaking to the staff.

'We have to hurry,' Aria whispered, her voice tight with urgency. 'They're going to use him to find the relic. We can't let them.'

Grandma looked up; her eyes sharp. 'If they get that relic, they'll have the power to open the gateway between worlds, and that would be catastrophic. We must get to Jayden before they do, but we can't just run in blind.'

Aria nodded, but her mind was still racing. The vision of Jayden's near-capture played over and over in her head. The vampires had been close, too close. They knew he was onto something, and they wouldn't hesitate to take him if they caught him again.

'Are you ready for this, dear?' Elleira asked, fastening her cloak around her shoulders, the fabric shimmering with a magical glow.

Aria nodded, her heart racing. 'I just keep thinking about what it will be like after we rescue Jayden. It feels like it's all I've wanted for so long.'

Elleira paused, sensing the bittersweet tone in Aria's voice. 'And what do you see in your mind, child?'

Aria took a deep breath, her eyes shimmering with unshed tears. 'I imagine us laughing together, sharing stories about our adventure. But...' She hesitated, glancing away. 'I just wish our parents were here to celebrate with us.'

Elleira's expression softened. 'I understand, dear. It's hard to think of them not being a part of this. But remember, they're with you in spirit, always.'

Aria managed a small smile. 'Yeah, I know. It just feels different without them.'

With a firm nod, Elleira stepped toward the door, her resolve unwavering. 'We will bring Jayden back, Aria. Together. Now, are you ready for the battle ahead?' Aria nodded firmly.

'But how can we find him?' Aria asked, her voice shaking. 'I don't know where he is now. He could be anywhere in that forest, and the vampires are faster than us. We'll never make it in time.'

'Of course we would,' Grandma reassured, her voice steady. 'We just have to stay strong.'

They hurried down the now familiar path, the forest around them buzzing with the whispers of leaves and distant rustling.

Yet, the massive tree ahead loomed as if it was a delusion, stubbornly refusing to draw any closer despite their frantic pace. It felt as if time itself had planned against them, stretching each step into an eternity.

'We're not getting any faster.' Elleira panted, her breath catching.

'Can't we just magic up a teleportation spell or something?' Aria asked desperately, her heart racing as she grasped for a quicker solution. Her mind whirled with possibilities, each one more unlikely than the last, but time was slipping away like sand through her fingers.

'Not that I can remember of,' Grandma replied gruffly. 'But I can turn our legs into wheels.'

'You can what?' she exclaimed incredulously, tinged with a hint of amusement.

'Trust me, it'll get us there faster.' Grandma insisted, a glimmer of mischief in her eyes.

Aria shot Elleira a sideways glance, a mix of scepticism and intrigue. 'I guess we're out of options.' said Aria, a reluctant smile tugging at her lips.

'Rotare Pedes.' Grandma said sharply, pointing her wand at Aria's feet. Aria felt an odd sensation, her legs stretching and twisting backward until they formed a circular shape.

'Rotare Pedes.' Grandma repeated, casting the same spell on herself. Her legs morphed similarly, but she looked perfectly normal, as if she'd done this countless times before.

'This is the weirdest spell we've ever tried.' Aria said with an amused tone, though it wasn't quite what she'd meant to express.

'An amusing spell, yes,' Elleira agreed, 'But necessary for serious matters.'

The once slow path now flew beneath them, their wheel-legs turning swiftly as though they were riding miniature cars.

After what felt like mere minutes, they arrived at the large, withered tree, where the coven stood, hoods lowered.

'Restituo Pedes,' Grandma said, casting the counter-spell to return Aria's legs to normal. Elleira did the same, her wheel-legs transforming back to feet.

'Turning your legs into wheels?' Phineas raised an eyebrow, smirking. 'Wow, what a groundbreaking idea! I mean, who needs actual teleportation when you can just roll in style?'

'We couldn't think of anything else.' Grandma said with a slight shrug.

'Focus, you two!' Alice interrupted, trying to steer the conversation back to business. 'We still need to prepare for the portal. The Spell of Passage requires both the truth serum and a protective circle.'

'Right,' Grandma said, pulling out a small vial filled with shimmering liquid from her satchel.

'This truth serum will ensure that anyone who steps through the portal does so with pure intentions. We can't afford any tricks, especially not from the vampires.' said Arthur.

'And the protective circle? How do we set that up?' asked Aria.

'Simple,' chirped Alice, 'Everyone, gather around.'

All the seven members gathered around in a circle. 'We have to tap our staffs seven times in unison,' said Reginald, as he went through the Grimoire, 'And the protection circle will follow us wherever we go.'

'What's the purpose of it?' asked Aria hastily, as she realised that they were running out of time.

'It acts as a temporary shield to us and is broken when we all are not within a particular range. So, everyone,' said Reginald, 'Tap your staffs seven times. On the count of three. One, two, three.'

The ground between Aria shook as the wizards tapped their wands seven times. Blue rays of light emitted from the top of the wand, forming detailed symbols, and the circle settled on the ground.

'Alright, everyone,' said Alice, 'Pass the vial, and drink only one drop of the truth serum.'

The coven members cautiously dripped one drop of the serum onto their mouth and swallowed it.

'Ready to open the portal?' asked Alice to the coven members, who nodded solemnly.

'I'll do the incantation,' volunteered Grandma, as she stepped forward, 'Get ready to face your truths.' she warned.

Grandma Elleira took a deep breath before she started the incantation.

'Par les racines et l'écorce,
Montre le chemin, par lumière ou ombre.
Montres le portail, délivre-nous.'

An irregular oval-like shape had appeared at the centre of the tree. Aria stood transfixed, staring at the shimmering portal that had appeared before them.

It was like looking into a rippling pool of water, only the surface showed a dark, shadowy world beyond—a world she knew her brother was trapped in.

She looked at the coven members for any sign of movement, but all were closing their eyes shut, as though experiencing pain and trauma.

Just as she was about to help them in some way (though she did not know what to do), they released themselves from their fixed posture and opened their eyes.

It was then she realised that they were forced to face their fears and truths.

'Is that it?' Aria whispered; her voice barely audible over the soft hum of the portal's energy.

'Yes,' said Gabrielle, her voice calm but tinged with urgency. 'This is our connection to the vampire world.

But remember this, child,' she warned, 'The vampire world is perilous. You must prepare yourselves for what lies ahead.'

Aria swallowed hard, nodding. 'Do we have a plan?'

Arthur took a deep breath. 'We'll only ferret around at first. We must find clues about where Jayden might be.'

Aria's heart pounded in her chest. The thought of seeing her brother again gave her strength, but the idea of walking into a world ruled by vampires filled her with dread.

'Ready?' Grandma asked Aria, her hand raised slightly, ready to lead them through the portal.

'As I'll ever be.' Aria whispered.

With one final glance at the world they were leaving behind, Aria stepped forward, her heart racing. Aria, Grandma and the coven walked one by one into the swirling blue portal, the cool energy wrapping around them as they passed through.

The world beyond was dark and cold. Shadows stretched long across the barren land, and a thick mist hung in the air. The air smelled faintly of damp earth and something metallic, like iron.

'This place...' Aria whispered, her voice shaking. 'It feels... alive.'

Grandma nodded. 'Stay close. We'll need to rely on each other now more than ever.'

As they ventured deeper into the vampire world, the eerie silence seemed to stretch on endlessly. Their footsteps echoed against the hard ground, and the further they walked, the heavier the air seemed to become. They didn't know what to expect, but the sense of being watched was overwhelming.

After what felt like hours, a low growl pierced the silence. Aria froze, her hand gripping Grandma's arm. 'What was that?'

Grandma's eyes darted around, scanning the shadows. 'We're not alone,' she murmured. 'Be ready.'

Suddenly, from the darkness, a pair of glowing red eyes appeared, followed by another set, and another. They were surrounded.

'Get behind me,' Grandma ordered, raising her wand. 'They're testing us.'

The creatures stepped forward into the faint light—their forms were humanoid but twisted, their skin pale, and their teeth sharp.

Aria's heart raced, but she held her ground. She wasn't going to back down now, not when they were so close.

One of the figures hissed, baring its fangs, but before it could move, Reginald pointed his wand directly at it and muttered an incantation under her breath. A burst of bright light shot from the tip of his wand, sending the creature stumbling back.

The other figures hesitated, their red eyes flickering with uncertainty. Alice's voice rang out, firm and unwavering. 'We're not here to fight. We seek passage.'

There was a moment of tense silence before one of the creatures spoke, its voice raspy and low. 'You are not welcome here, witches.'

Aria stepped forward, her heart pounding. 'We're here for my brother. We don't want trouble. Just let us find him and we'll leave.'

The creature's eyes flickered, as if considering her words. 'The boy is already lost. You cannot save him.'

Grandma's breath caught in her throat. 'You're lying.'

Persephone placed a hand on Aria's shoulder, her voice calm but firm. 'We know he's here, and we won't leave without him.'

The vampires melted into the shadows, their figures becoming indistinct as they slipped silently into the thick forest. One moment they were there, watching with their cold, predatory eyes, and the next, they were gone—vanishing without a sound, leaving only the rustle of leaves behind.

'Why did they go?' asked Aria to Persephone.

Just as Persephone was about to answer, a loud rustling noise erupted from behind them. Aria spun around; her eyes wide with alarm. Out of the shadows, a figure emerged, who looked like her brother.

'Jayden?' Aria gasped, running towards him. But something was off. His face was pale, his eyes distant. He didn't speak, just stared past her, almost as if he were in a trance.

Grandma moved quickly, placing herself between Aria and Jayden, her eyes narrowing with suspicion. 'This isn't right,' she muttered. 'He shouldn't be here.'

Aria looked back at the portal, which was still pulsing with light. 'Is this a trick?' she whispered.

Before Grandma could answer, Jayden's figure flickered, as though he were a mere projection. Then, without warning, he vanished into thin air.

'It's an illusion,' Reginald said grimly, lowering her wand. 'The vampire world is playing with us. They want to confuse us before we even step inside.'

Aria clenched her fists. 'Then we can't let them win. We need to go through and find the real Jayden.'

Grandma nodded; her eyes filled with resolve. 'Let's go.'

They moved through the trees, stepping into a place that felt strange and magical. The sky was completely black, with no stars, leaving the full moon as the only source of light.

Thick fog covered the ground, rising to their knees, making it look like they were walking on clouds. It felt like they were in a beautiful but creepy dream, with everything below looking calm, yet the sky above felt heavy and threatening.

The fog was so thick that they could barely see their feet, and the air felt cold and still. It seemed peaceful on the ground, but there was something scary in the atmosphere, like danger was lurking just out of sight.

They continued through the eerie fog until, abruptly, they reached a dead end. A tall wall of thick, twisted vines blocked their path, and there didn't seem to be any way forward. Aria's heart sank.

'We're stuck,' she said, frustration creeping into her voice. The coven members fanned out, searching the area for any clue that could lead them ahead.

Gabrielle's sharp eyes landed on something half-buried in the misty ground. 'Over here,' she called, bending down. She unearthed a small, ancient-looking box, its surface covered in cryptic symbols.

Aria knelt beside her, tracing the intricate carvings with her fingers. 'There's a lock, but no keyhole.'

Gabrielle examined it closely, her eyes narrowing. 'It's a puzzle. We'll have to crack the code.'

Everyone gathered around, their breaths clouding in the cold air as they stared at the box. Phineas was the first to speak. 'There's something familiar about this design...' He paused, studying the symbols more closely. 'This is a vampire's crest.'

Aria's eyes widened. 'We have to draw the vampire's symbol to unlock it?'

Arthur nodded grimly. 'It's part of their dark magic. They protect their secrets fiercely, and only those who know their symbols can access it.'

Alice stepped forward, holding out a piece of chalk. 'We'll need to draw the crest on the ground,' she said, her voice steady. 'But it has to be exact, or the spell will fail.'

With careful hands, they began to trace the vampire crest on the ground—sharp lines and curves that interlocked in a way that seemed to pulse with ancient power. The fog swirled around them as the symbol took shape, the air growing colder with each stroke.

When the last line was drawn, the box clicked open with a quiet snap.

They all held their breath as the lid slowly lifted. Inside was a key—black and sleek, glinting ominously in the moonlight.

Aria exchanged a glance with Grandma. 'This must be it. The way forward.'

With the key in hand, they turned back toward the wall of vines. Grandma approached it cautiously, the key clutched tightly in her hand. The rest of the coven stood behind her, watching as she examined the wall, searching for a keyhole or some kind of opening.

'This is it.' Grandma muttered, squinting at a small, almost invisible indentation in the thick vines. She slid the key into the hidden lock, and with a soft click, the vines began to unravel, slowly parting like a curtain.

Beyond the vines, a large stone archway stood, its surface covered in more symbols—ancient runes glowing faintly in the moonlight.

'Let's go.' said Grandma.

In the centre stood a large, ancient stone structure, half-hidden by the mist. The air around it felt charged with dark magic, and the very sight of it sent a chill down Aria's spine.

Aria swallowed hard, her eyes scanning the ancient building. 'Are you sure Jayden's in there?'

Grandma nodded, her face tense. 'I can feel his presence. But this place is protected by powerful magic. We'll have to be careful.'

They approached the entrance, a large, arched doorway carved into the stone. As they stepped closer, Aria noticed strange symbols etched into the stone around the door—symbols that pulsed faintly with an ominous glow.

Grandma took a deep breath and turned to Aria and the coven. 'This is it. Once we go inside, there's no turning back.'

Aria nodded, her stomach twisting with nerves. But she wasn't going to hesitate now. 'Let's go.'

Together, they stepped through the doorway and into the dark interior of the structure. The air inside was heavy with the scent of damp stone and something else—something metallic and sharp, like blood.

They reached a large chamber. At the far end of the room, Aria saw him—Jayden, bound by glowing chains, sitting against the cold stone wall.

'Jayden!' Aria cried, rushing forward.

But before she could reach him, a figure stepped out of the shadows—a tall, pale vampire with piercing eyes and a cold, cruel smile. His presence seemed to fill the room with a chilling darkness.

'You've come a long way,' the vampire said, his voice smooth and mocking. 'But you're too late. The boy is already ours.'

Persephone stepped forward, her fingers gripping the staff defensively. 'He doesn't belong to you,' she said, her voice firm. 'Release him.'

The vampire laughed, a cold, mirthless sound. 'You're brave, witch, but foolish. The boy's soul is bound to this place. If you want him back, you'll have to offer something in return.'

Aria's heart raced. 'What do you want?'

The vampire's eyes gleamed. 'A life for a life. His freedom in exchange for yours.'

Aria felt the blood drain from her face. 'You mean... me?'

'Don't listen to him,' Reginald warned, stepping protectively in front of Aria. 'There's always another way.'

The vampire's smile widened. 'Is there? You're in my domain now, and I make the rules.'

For a moment, the room was deathly still, the weight of the vampire's demand hanging in the air.

But then, Grandma's voice cut through the silence. 'You forget, we're not powerless here.'

With a swift motion, Grandma pointed her staff at the vampire and began to chant a powerful spell.

'Incutio!' yelled Grandma.

The vampire was blasted backward. His smile faltered, and he hissed in anger. 'You'll regret this, witch!' He lunged at Elleira, but Arthur cast a spell, knocking the vampire aside.

All at once, the room exploded into chaos.

Vampires lunged forward, their claws extended, and fangs bared. But the witches were ready. Persephone shouted an incantation, and a blast of bright green streak erupted from her staff, sending a group of vampires flying across the chamber. Reginald followed suit, his staff casting a net of shimmering silver light that trapped several vampires in place, their snarls muffled by the magical barrier.

'Salva Guardo!' Alice cried, as a protective shield emerged between Aria and the coven.

Grandma was already in motion. With a tap of her staff, she sent a barrage of fiery orbs spinning toward the approaching vampires. 'Don't let them get close!' she shouted over the noise of the battle.

Reginald and Gabrielle fought side by side, their spells harmonising perfectly. As Reginald summoned bolts of lightning that struck vampires down with precision, Gabrielle created whirlwinds of magic that disoriented their foes, sending them stumbling in every direction.

'Arthur, the east wall!' Alice yelled, noticing a group of vampires attempting to flank them.

Arthur turned sharply, his eyes narrowing. 'On it.' He tapped his staff, and a wave of dark spirals erupted from the ground, ensnaring the vampires before they could get any closer. The creatures shrieked and struggled, but Arthur's magic held them firmly in place.

Suddenly, a figure darted toward Aria with blinding speed—a vampire with glowing red eyes, faster and more vicious than the others. Before Aria could react, the vampire crashed into her protective barrier, shattering it with a deafening crack. She stumbled back, fear surging through her as the vampire closed in.

'Aria!' Grandma's voice rang out, and before the vampire could strike, a burst of light from Persephone's wand distracted the vampire.

'Stay focused!' Persephone called to Elleira, 'They won't stop until we're all drained dry.'

Elleira nodded, gearing herself. The coven was holding their ground, but the sheer number of vampires seemed overwhelming. For every vampire they struck down, more seemed to appear, crawling out of the shadows and hissing with fury.

Reginald, sweat on his forehead, looked at Arthur. 'We need to end this fast!' he shouted over the din. 'They're drawing power from this place—it's like an endless supply of them!'

Arthur's face tightened with realisation. He raised his wand and pointed toward the ceiling of the chamber, where the strange, glowing runes pulsed with dark energy. 'It's the runes,' he said, his voice grim. 'They're keeping the portal to the vampire world open, letting more of them through.'

Without hesitation, Arthur raised his staff higher. 'Persephone, Gabrielle—help me disrupt the magic!'

Persephone and Gabrielle nodded, positioning themselves beside Arthur. The three began chanting in unison, their voices rising above the chaos of the battle.

Their staff glowed with blinding light as they directed their magic toward the ceiling.

The effect was immediate. The glowing runes began to flicker, their light sputtering as the witches' magic clashed with the dark energy of the portal. The ground beneath them rumbled, and the vampires, sensing the disruption, howled in rage.

'Keep them off us!' Arthur shouted to the rest of the coven as he and the others focused on the runes.

Grandma, now fully in the fight, casting stunning spells at any vampire that dared approach, while Aria was still in the protective barrier, trying to shield herself in a crouched position, though she knew that it would not help when any one of the vampires attacked her.

Meanwhile, with every passing second, the runes' light grew dimmer.

Reginald, with a fierce battle cry, unleashed a torrent of flame that engulfed the last group of vampires charging toward him. 'It's working!' he yelled, watching as fewer and fewer vampires emerged from the shadows.

Finally, with a deafening crack, the runes above them shattered. The chamber was filled with a pulse of energy as the portal to the vampire world collapsed in on itself.

The remaining vampires shrieked in agony as their connection to the runes was severed. One by one, they began to disintegrate into dust, their forms crumbling away until nothing remained.

The silence that followed was almost deafening. The once-chaotic chamber was now eerily still, the only sound the breathing of the witches and wizards who had fought so hard.

Aria collapsed to her knees, exhausted but relieved. They had done it—they had won.

Grandma approached her, placing a comforting hand on her shoulder. 'You did well,' she said softly. 'We all did.'

The rest of the coven gathered around; their faces worn but triumphant. Persephone gave a weary smile, her staff still glowing faintly. 'Well, that was... intense.'

Reginald chuckled, wiping sweat from his forehead. 'Let's never do that again.'

Aria couldn't help but smile, though her thoughts quickly turned to Jayden, still bound in the corner. 'We need to free him,' she said, standing up shakily.

Grandma nodded. 'Let's get him out of here. The battle may be over, but there's still work to do.'

As Aria hurried toward Jayden, the tension in her body began to ease. The vampires were gone and victory seemed within their grasp. But as she got closer, something strange caught her attention.

Jayden, who had been slumped against the wall, bound by rusted chains, didn't move or show any sign of relief. He didn't even seem to breathe.

'Jayden?' Aria called cautiously, her voice echoing in the now-empty chamber.

Grandma, who had been beside her moments before, narrowed her eyes, sensing something off. 'Aria, wait...' she warned, but Aria had already reached out, her fingers brushing against his shoulder.

The moment she touched him, the image of Jayden flickered like a mirage. Her heart lurched as the figure blurred and shimmered, revealing the truth.

Jayden wasn't real. He was an illusion, nothing more than a magical projection.

'No!' Aria gasped, stumbling back. Her mind raced, her thoughts spinning in disbelief. 'It can't be... we saw him...'

'Can't believe we fell for that old trick *again*.' scowled Reginald.

The entire coven gathered around, their faces showing varying levels of shock and confusion. 'An illusion spell of this magnitude—it was designed to trick us from the beginning.' said Persephone.

'But why?' asked Arthur, his voice low and steady as he stepped closer, examining the remnants of the illusion as it dissipated into the air. 'And where's the real Jayden?'

Persephone's eyes darkened with realisation. 'This was a trap. Whoever created this illusion wanted to lure us here, to keep us occupied while they carried out their real plan.'

'Then they could still have him!' Aria said, her voice trembling with a mixture of fear and anger. She turned to Grandma, her eyes pleading. 'We must find him. We can't stop now!'

Grandma's expression was grim, but resolute. 'We will. But whoever did this have powerful magic. They've been several steps ahead of us all along.'

Gabrielle, who had been unusually quiet, spoke up. 'They wanted us to waste time fighting them while Jayden was moved somewhere else.'

Alice nodded in agreement. 'That makes sense. They weren't fighting to win—they were just keeping us distracted.'

Reginald clenched his fists, frustration evident on his face. 'So, where is he now? And how do we find him?'

Aria's heart pounded as she looked around the chamber, searching for any clue that might give them a lead. 'There must be something here—a trace of where they took him.'

Persephone raised her staff and began to chant a revealing spell. 'Revelare,' said Persephone, and the air in the room shimmered once more as glowing symbols appeared on the stone walls—marks of a spell far more complex than they'd anticipated.

'It's a cloaking ritual,' Persephone said, tracing her fingers over the faint symbols. 'And a powerful one. Whoever did this didn't just hide Jayden—they've hidden their entire presence.'

'Then how do we break through it?' Aria asked, her voice urgent.

Grandma stepped forward, her eyes focused and determined. 'There is one way,' she said, her voice steady but laced with caution. 'But it requires immense magical focus from all of us. We need to trace the person who did the illusion. If we can pinpoint the source, we can follow it to wherever Jayden is being held.'

'Let's do it,' Alice said without hesitation. 'Whatever it takes.'

The coven quickly formed a circle again, their staff raised high. Aria could feel the weight of the moment pressing down on her, but she pushed her fear aside. They had come this far—they couldn't fail now.

As the witches and wizards began chanting, their voices harmonising in the air, the symbols on the walls glowed brighter. Slowly, the dark magic revealed, showing threads of power that led out of the chamber.

'There,' said Grandma, her voice tight with concentration. 'We've got the trail. Now, we must follow it.'

But as the magic revealed further, the trail began to twist and turn, leading into a vast, shadowy tunnel beyond the chamber's reach. Aria's pulse quickened, and an overwhelming sense of urgency washed over her. She could almost feel Jayden's presence tugging at her soul, distant but alive. There was no time to lose the soul.

Persephone's forehead furrowed as she stared at the magical threads. 'It's not going to be easy. They've masked his location well, and these magic feels... ancient.'

Grandma's face remained resolute. 'Ancient or not, we're going after him.' She turned to the coven. 'Stay sharp. This may be a trap, but we've faced worse.'

Without another word, they followed the trail, moving deeper into the complicated tunnels beneath the vampire world.

The walls were cold and damp, and the air smelled of earth and old magic. The deeper they went, the stronger the oppressive energy became, pressing down on their senses.

As they ventured further, the magical threads led them to a large iron door, heavy and worn with age. Aria felt a chill run down her spine. The door seemed to hum with dark energy, and faint whispers echoed from the other side.

Reginald stepped forward, placing his hand on the door. 'Here we are. The magic is concentrated here.'

'Be ready,' warned Alice, her wand gripped tightly in her hand. 'Whoever set this up might be waiting for us on the other side.'

Grandma gave a nod, her face set in determination. 'Let's break this barrier.'

Together, the coven raised their staff and yelled, 'Propatulus!'.

The iron door shook as their magic surged against it, cracks of light spreading across its surface. With a final burst of energy, the door exploded inward, revealing a vast courtyard beyond.

Inside, the atmosphere was different—thicker, darker, filled with a suffocating sense of dread. The yard was bathed in shadows, and at its centre stood a raised stone altar, draped in crimson cloth.

And there, under a zapped orb, with orange and purple hues, bound to the relic, was Jayden.

Aria's heart leaped at the sight of him, but her relief quickly turned to horror. Standing around the altar were figures cloaked in dark robes, their faces obscured, their eyes glowing with unnatural light.

Vampires—and not just any vampires. These were the leaders, the true masterminds behind the illusion.

The tallest of them stepped forward, his face finally visible under the flickering torchlight. He smiled, revealing sharp fangs that gleamed menacingly. 'You've come far, little witches,' he said, his voice smooth and cold. 'But you're too late.'

Grandma's staff snapped up instinctively, her eyes blazing with fury. 'Let him go!'

The vampire leader chuckled darkly. 'Oh, we will. But not until we've finished our ritual.' He gestured to Jayden, who lay unconscious on the altar, his chest rising and falling shallowly. 'You see, Jayden's blood is the key to unlocking a power far beyond your comprehension. And with the portal to the vampire realm closed, we need... alternatives.'

Arthur's eyes narrowed; his staff pointed directly at the vampire leader. 'We're not giving you the chance.'

The battle erupted instantly. The vampires moved with unnatural speed, darting through the air as they clashed with the witches' magic. Spells flew in every direction, illuminating the chamber with flashes of blue and red.

Grandma focused all her energy on the vampire leader, her wand crackling with raw power. She sent a blast of energy toward him, but he easily sidestepped it, moving with a fluidity that made him seem like a shadow.

'You'll have to do better than that,' he sneered, his voice echoing through the yard.

But Elleira was relentless. She fired spell after spell, each one narrowly missing as the vampire leader danced around her attacks. The others were locked in their own battles, trying to keep the vampires from reaching Jayden, who remained unconscious on the altar.

Aria, meanwhile, had her sights set on the ritual itself. She noticed the dark runes etched into the altar's stone surface, glowing faintly with the same ancient magic they had seen earlier. She knew that if they didn't stop the ritual soon, Jayden would be lost.

'Reginald, cover me!' Phineas called out, rushing toward the altar.

Reginald nodded, casting a barrier around them as Phineas began to chant a counterspell. The dark runes flickered and sparked as her magic clashed with the vampire's ritual.

Grandma, still locked in her duel with the vampire leader, felt a surge of anger and desperation. With a fierce shout, she unleashed a powerful blast of magic that finally caught the vampire off guard, sending him crashing into the stone wall with a thunderous impact.

Taking advantage of the moment, Aria ran to Jayden's side, her hands trembling as she placed them on his chest. He was still breathing, but barely. 'Jayden, please wake up,' she whispered, tears welling in her eyes.

Suddenly, a sharp laugh echoed through the yard, and Aria looked up to see the vampire leader standing, his face twisted in rage. 'You think you've won?' he snarled. 'This is far from over.'

Before anyone could react, the vampire leader raised his hand, and the air in the yard crackled with dark energy. The ground began to shake violently, and from the shadows, something massive stirred.

A hulking figure emerged—a monstrous vampire creature, twice the size of any they had faced before, its eyes glowing with malevolent hunger. It roared, the sound shaking the very foundations of the chamber, and charged toward them.

"Get back!" Grandma Elleira's voice rang out with urgent authority as she thrust her arms forward, conjuring a shimmering, translucent shield that enveloped Aria and Jayden just in time.

The creature's massive, clawed hand slammed into the barrier with a bone-rattling force, sending bright, crackling ripples through the air. Aria could feel the weight of the impact vibrate through her bones, but the shield held firm.

From the corner of her eye, she saw Phineas, Persephone, and Arthur position themselves, their wands raised in unison. Without hesitation, they shouted, "Obstupefio!" in perfect harmony.

Bright streaks of magic shot forward, converging in a beam of concentrated energy that struck the hulking vampire square in the chest. The effect was immediate. The creature, towering and fierce, staggered, its feral eyes wide with shock.

For a moment, time seemed to stretch, and then—crack. The vampire's massive body began to tremble violently.

In less than three seconds, the ground beneath them trembled as the giant vampire collapsed with a thunderous crash, sending a cloud of dust and debris into the air. The earth itself seemed to quake malevolently under its weight, as if recoiling from the evil presence that had just been felled.

Grandma dodged another vampire's strike, casting a defensive spell that sent her attacker flying backward. The others were fighting fiercely, but the vampires, now bolstered by the lunar power, were relentless. Their speed and strength had increased by ten times, and the coven was struggling to keep up.

'This is getting out of control!' Persephone shouted over the din of battle; her voice strained as she blocked an attack with a shield spell. 'They're feeding off the moon! If we don't stop them, they'll become unstoppable!'

Grandma, who was near the altar with Reginald, was deep in concentration, still chanting the counterspell to break the ritual's hold on Jayden. But the dark runes on the stone glowed brighter with each passing second, the vampires' connection to the moon strengthening.

Aria knew they had to disrupt the flow of energy. She turned her gaze to the moon, narrowing her eyes. 'We have to damage their link to the moon's power! If we can break the connection, they'll lose their advantage!'

'How?' Reginald shouted, casting a lightning bolt at a nearby vampire, who dodged it with supernatural speed.

Aria's mind raced. The vampires were drawing energy from the moon through the symbols etched into the ground—a massive circle of runes that radiated out from the altar. If they could destroy the runes, they might break the connection.

She rushed toward the closest rune. 'We need to break these!' she yelled, pointing to the symbols on the ground. 'Everyone, focus on the runes!'

Persephone caught on immediately, hurling a fire spell at one of the glowing symbols. The rune shattered under the force of the magic, sending a pulse of energy rippling through the air. The nearest vampire hissed in pain as the connection to the moon weakened slightly.

Encouraged, Elleira unleashed her magic on the next rune, the light from her spell bursting across the ground and breaking the symbol apart. All around her, the coven was doing the same, focusing their attacks on the runes that fuelled the vampires' power.

But the vampires weren't going to let their advantage slip away easily. The vampire leader, his eyes glowing a deep crimson, let out a furious roar. 'You think you can stop us? We are the children of the night! The moon belongs to us!'

He raised his hands toward the sky, and the moon's light intensified, casting long, menacing shadows across the courtyard. The vampires surged forward with renewed fury, their movements a blur as they fought to protect the remaining runes.

One of them lunged at Aria, his claws outstretched. She barely managed to dodge, rolling to the side, while Gabrielle shot him with an attacking spell, but he shook it off like it was nothing. The moonlight had made them nearly invincible.

'Keep going!' Phineas shouted, his voice breaking through the chaos. 'We're almost there!'

Gabrielle gritted her teeth and pressed on, blasting another rune with her magic. The ground beneath her shook as the energy lines between the vampires and the moon began to flicker and weaken.

The vampires' movements became less coordinated, their supernatural speed started to slow down.

But the leader was relentless. He bared his fangs and summoned a towering wall of shadows to protect the last few runes. 'You won't destroy our power!' he bellowed, his voice echoing across the courtyard.

Aria's heart raced. They were running out of time. If the vampires completed the ritual, Jayden would be lost, and the coven might not survive the night.

Suddenly, a flash of insight struck her. The vampires' connection to the moon was being drawn from both the symbols and the leader himself. He was acting as the source, passing the moon's energy into the others. If they could disrupt him directly, the entire flow would collapse.

'Grandma! Persephone! We need to take him out!' Aria shouted, pointing at the vampire leader. 'He's the source!'

The witches exchanged tense glances, their eyes silently communicating the urgency of the moment. In perfect synchronization, they raised their arms, their voices melding into one as they chanted, "Friguso!" A shimmering wave of icy blue magic shot forth from their hands, engulfing the leader of their enemies in a swirl of frost. He stood completely still, a statue of frozen rage.

Just as the witches caught their breath, Reginald's voice boomed through the air, filled with raw power. "Displodo!" The force of his spell rippled across the yard, a shockwave of energy that collided with the frozen figure. With a deafening crack, the leader was flung aside like a ragdoll, tumbling through the air before crashing hard into the ground.

As the vampire leader fell, the connection to the moon snapped like a broken thread. The remaining vampires let out agonised shrieks as the lunar energy was ripped from their bodies, leaving them weakened and disoriented.

Aria didn't hesitate. She sprinted toward the altar, followed by Grandma, whose staff was cackling with power. With a final, desperate chant, she released a surge of magic that shattered the remaining runes, breaking the vampires' hold on the ritual for good.

The moonlight dimmed, and the courtyard was plunged into eerie silence. Jayden, still lying on the altar, let out a soft groan as the dark magic holding him captive began to fade.

Aria rushed to his side, her heart pounding in her chest. 'Jayden,' she whispered, her hand gently resting on his forehead. His skin was cool to the touch, but colour was returning to his cheeks. Slowly, his eyes fluttered open.

'Aria?' His voice was weak, but alive.

Tears of relief welled up in her eyes. 'You're okay. We've got you.' she replied, her voice shaking with emotion. Without thinking, she leaned down and enveloped him in a tight hug, feeling his warmth against her.

Jayden, still weak, managed to lift his arms and return the embrace, holding her tightly as if she were his anchor. 'I was so scared,' he confessed, his voice barely above a whisper.

Aria pulled back just enough to look into his eyes, her heart swelling with love and concern. 'I know, but you're safe now. We're going to get you out of here,' she reassured him, brushing a stray hair from his face.

He smiled faintly, despite the pain he was in. 'Thanks for coming for me. I thought... I thought I wouldn't see you again.'

Her heart ached at his words, and she tightened her grip around him, refusing to let go. 'You're not getting rid of me that easily,' she said with a soft chuckle, though it was tinged with relief. 'We're a team, remember? I'll always find you.'

Behind them, the vampires were retreating, too weakened to continue the fight. The vampire leader, still on the ground, glared at them with hatred, but his power was broken.

Grandma approached, her wand still glowing faintly. 'It's over,' she said softly. 'We've won.'

The night air was cool and still, the threat finally passed. But as Aria looked up at the fading moon, she knew that their battle against the dark forces that sought to control the world was far from over.

The coven left the courtyard, which lay in ruins from the devastating clash of spells. The once vibrant space was now littered with shattered stones, charred grass, and a lingering mist of magical energy.

Without a word, they began their walk toward the ancient tree—the passage between two worlds. As they approached, the air grew colder, the boundary between realms vibrating with a power only they could feel.

Aria, still clutching Jayden's hand tightly, couldn't help but glance at him every few seconds. The fear that had gripped her for so long was slowly dissolving, replaced by overwhelming relief.

She had him back. After everything—the sleepless nights, the constant worry, the unimaginable battle—they were together again.

Jayden looked over at her and gave a weak smile, his expression tired but peaceful. His eyes spoke volumes of the gratitude and love he felt. Aria pulled him closer, resting her head briefly on his shoulder as they continued to walk toward the tree.

It was the kind of silence between them that didn't need words—just the comfort of knowing they were no longer alone.

The tree loomed ahead, towering over them with its ancient branches reaching high into the sky, twisting as if they knew the secrets of both worlds. The portal shimmered faintly, waiting for the final spell to close it once more.

As Grandma and the others began their incantation, Aria and Jayden stood off to the side, watching. For a moment, they simply looked at each other, taking in the reality of what had happened. Aria's heart ached with a mixture of relief and exhaustion. She felt like she could breathe again, truly breathe, for the first time in what felt like forever.

Jayden reached out, wrapping his arms around her in a tight embrace. She hugged him back, not wanting to let go. The warmth of his presence was all she needed; all she had wanted for so long.

Aria could feel the weight of everything lifting from her shoulders. The world, which had been so terrifying and uncertain, seemed almost normal again, at least for now.

The tree behind them glowed one final time, and with a low hum, the portal sealed shut. The connection between the worlds was severed, at least for now. They were safe.

Aria and Jayden shared a glance, a silent agreement passing between them.

It was over. They were going home. Together.

But as they walked, a hollow ache settled in—this was a moment their parents would never get to see.

CHAPTER TWELVE

Light at Last

As they made their way back through the forest, Jayden's footsteps slowed, a heaviness weighing him down.

Aria noticed and stopped, turning to face him with concern. 'Jayden, are you okay?' she asked, her voice soft in the quiet night. 'You don't seem... relieved that we saved you.'

Jayden's eyes flickered with an unreadable emotion. He sighed and ran a hand through his unkempt hair, avoiding her gaze. 'Aria, there's something I need to tell you.' His tone was distant, and suddenly, it felt like a wall had sprung up between them.

Aria frowned, stepping closer. 'What do you mean? You were captured, taken for some kind of twisted ritual. We saved you, Jayden.' She noticed that the coven was hearing their conversation too.

Jayden shook his head, his jaw tightening. 'I wasn't just captured. I went to them... willingly.'

The words hit Aria like a punch to the chest. She stared at him, bewildered. 'What? Why would you—'

'I needed answers,' Jayden interrupted, his voice firm but laced with regret. 'I discovered my connection to magic a few months ago, long before any of this started. I started noticing... things. I didn't want to put anyone in danger but myself. I thought I could handle it all on my own, and—' He broke off, and Aria noticed tears welling in his eyes.

'Shh, it's alright,' Aria soothed. 'We saved you in time—that's what matters.'

A silence followed, filled with the joyful whispers of Grandma and the coven, who were ecstatic to witness the bond between the twins, one of whom had been lost.

'Look at them! They look so happy together!' chirped Alice.

'Just look at the adorable baby-boos,' cooed Gabrielle. Jayden and Aria exchanged glances, struggling hard not to make a pucker face. Grandma Elleira smirked at them, clearly knowing their discomfort at being called 'baby-boos'.

'Reminds me of how close Maria and Arielle were.' added Reginald.

Grandma turned to him. 'That was friendship. This is something deeper—it's siblinghood. It's family.'

'Couldn't agree more,' Phineas added, nodding in agreement.

The rest of them acknowledged each other with a nod. The mood shifted slightly, the playful teasing giving way to a more serious tone.

The coven members, sensing the weight of the moment, quieted down, their focus turning back to Jayden. The trees around them rustled softly in the wind, adding to the atmosphere.

'So, Jay, how did you know about the vampires?' Aria asked gently, her eyes searching his face.

Jayden took a deep breath, as though he had expected this question, his eyes darting to the moonlit forest around them before settling back on Aria. His hesitation hung in the air for a moment, then he began speaking, his voice laced with a sense of wariness.

'It started about a year ago,' Jayden began, kicking at the ground as if unsure how to explain. 'Remember the time when you were sick and me and Uncle Harold for a hike in the woods behind the old quarry—you know, the one we used to talk about exploring?' Aria nodded.

'Well, one day I went farther than usual. There was this weird mist in the air, like something out of a dream. I thought it was just the weather, but it wasn't normal. The air felt... thick, almost like something was watching me.'

Aria listened intently; her curiosity piqued as Jayden continued.

'I stumbled upon this old clearing, deep in the forest. It wasn't on any of the trails on the map. There was this huge, ancient-looking stone circle, almost like a monument. At first, I thought it was some abandoned historical site or something. But then, I heard voices. That's when I saw them—vampires.'

His words sent a chill down Aria's spine.

'And the stone circle was the relic, wasn't it?' asked Arthur. Jayden nodded.

'They were standing in the circle,' Jayden went on, his voice growing more intense as he recalled the memory. 'I hid behind some trees and watched them from a distance. They were performing some sort of ritual. There was a bright silver light emitting from the centre of the stone circle, and they were drawing energy from it. The leader, this tall vampire with glowing red eyes, was chanting something, and the others were standing in formation, like they were pulling power from the moon itself.'

Aria's eyes widened. 'You saw them... performing a ritual?'

Jayden nodded. 'Yeah. At first, I didn't believe what I was seeing. I thought maybe it was some weird cult. But then... the leader sensed me. He stopped in the middle of the ritual, looked directly at the spot where I was hiding, and smiled. It was like he could smell my fear. I panicked and ran before they could get to me, but from that moment, I knew something wasn't right.'

Aria took a deep breath. 'So that's how you first found out about them. But why didn't you tell anyone?'

Jayden shrugged, his face tightening with guilt. 'I was scared. What would I even say? 'Hey, I just saw a bunch of vampires in the woods performing some sort of ritual'?

No one would've believed me. I barely believed it myself. But I couldn't let it go. I kept going back to the woods, trying to find answers. I researched everything I could about the vampires—their history, their weaknesses, their rituals. I found ancient texts, hidden forums online, even secret records buried in the local archives.'

Aria blinked in surprise. 'Local archives?'

'Yeah,' Jayden nodded. 'Turns out there were old records about strange happenings in this area dating back centuries. People disappearing, reports of strange figures wandering the woods at night—it all added up. It was all connected to the vampires. And that circle I saw? It's been a place of power for them for hundreds of years; which is why they needed me to be sacrificed to renew the power.'

Gabrielle, who had been quietly listening, finally spoke up. 'You found the heart of their power, didn't you? That circle—the relic, is part of the vampire's binding to this land. It's how they draw strength from the moon.'

Jayden nodded again. 'Exactly. I kept digging and found out about their plans. They wanted to take control of the whole world. They had to perform a complex ritual for that. They needed someone who knows their secrets, someone they could use to finish their ritual without interference.'

Aria's heart raced. 'That's why they took you. You knew too much.'

Jayden ran a hand through his hair, exhaling shakily. 'Yeah. I thought if I confronted them, I could stop them, maybe warn someone. But they were smarter than I gave them credit for. They lured me into a trap, and I didn't even realise it until it was too late. They wanted to use me—use my knowledge of their world—against anyone who would try to stop them.'

Persephone stepped forward; her eyes sharp with understanding. 'And that's why they took you,' she said softly. 'Not because you have magic, but because you knew their secrets. They needed to silence you... or use your knowledge to their advantage.'

Jayden nodded, his face pale in the moonlight. 'Yeah. They knew I'd seen too much, and when I tried to confront them, they turned the tables on me. I didn't realise how powerful they were.'

Aria's heart sank as she pieced it together. Jayden had been in danger this whole time, not because of some latent magic but because he had stumbled into the vampire world by pure chance—and because he had been trying to protect her, even if he had gone about, it the wrong way.

Aria stood still, absorbing his words, her mind racing. 'So, you've known all along?' she asked, her voice quieter now. 'About the vampires, about the danger... and you never said anything about it to me?'

Jayden's face twisted with regret. 'I didn't know how to tell you, Aria. I didn't even understand what was happening to me. I thought I could figure it out on my own, that maybe the vampires had answers I couldn't find anywhere else. But I was wrong.'

Aria's fists clenched, frustration boiling inside her. 'Why didn't you just come to us first? We could've helped you, Jayden. We've been through so much together. You didn't have to do this alone.'

Jayden looked at her, guilt and sorrow in his eyes. 'I thought I was protecting you. I didn't want you to get hurt because of something I couldn't control.'

'Or you could have called me while you were researching, right?'

Jayden rubbed the back of his neck, looking a bit sheepish. 'I guess I didn't want to worry you. I thought it would be safer to figure it all out on my own first. And honestly, I wasn't sure how you'd react to all this—if you'd even believe me.'

Aria softened, her initial anger melting into concern. 'Jayden, you don't have to do this alone. You should've trusted me. We could've helped you.' said Aria again.

Grandma Elleira nodded. 'This world, the one you stumbled into, is dangerous for anyone—magical or not. The vampires thrive on secrecy, and knowing what you do makes you a threat to them. But you're with us now, and we'll keep you safe.'

Jayden looked up; his eyes filled with relief but also lingering guilt. 'I didn't realise how much danger I was in until it was too late. I'm sorry, Aria. I thought I could protect you... I thought I could protect everyone.'

Aria stepped closer, putting a hand on his arm. 'You're not alone in this, Jayden. We face these dangers together. No more secrets, okay?'

Jayden managed a small smile, nodding. 'No more secrets.'

They reached the end of the forest, standing at the Enchanted Summit, where the air buzzed with a mix of magic and anticipation. It was time to exchange goodbyes, and the atmosphere was heavy with emotions.

Aria stepped forward, her heart swelling with gratitude. 'Thank you all for doing this for me. For us. I don't exactly know how I can thank you, but I will try to make up for it someday.' Her voice trembled slightly, the weight of their sacrifices pressing upon her.

Alice, the youngest member of the coven, stepped up beside her. 'You don't need to worry about that, Aria. We're just glad to see you both safe. That's what family does!' She flashed a bright smile, her eyes sparkling with warmth.

Persephone nodded in agreement, brushing a stray hair from her face. 'Exactly! Just knowing we helped makes it all worthwhile. Plus, we'll always be here if you need us again. We're like your magical backup crew!'

Phineas chimed in with a playful grin, 'And if you ever find yourself in another pickle, remember we're just a spell away. No more vampire encounters, okay?'

Aria chuckled, the tension easing a bit. 'Deal! No more vampire trouble. I'll stick to a boring, normal life from now on—if I can help it.'

Reginald stepped forward; his expression serious but kind. 'You've shown great courage today, Aria. Just remember that strength is not just about power; it's about having the heart to fight for those you love. You and Jayden have that in common.'

Gabrielle stepped forward, pulling Aria into a warm embrace. 'We believe in you, dear. Never forget that. You have a family here who will always stand by you.'

'You have given us another experience. Truly to say, it's been many years since we had fought a battle—and it felt great. So, a bunch of thanks to you, Aria,' said Arthur. Aria smiled at him.

Elleira joined them. 'Thank you, everyone. Seriously. We couldn't have done this without you.'

With one last wave and heartfelt smiles, the coven began to disperse, each member retreating into the shadows of the forest, leaving Aria and Jayden feeling a profound sense of connection and hope for the future.

CHAPTER THIRTEEN

The Curtain Falls

The walk to Grandma's shop was slow and quiet. The snap of twigs, which Aria had once found oddly satisfying, now felt meaningless. The only thing on her mind was the fact that her brother was right here with her—it felt surreal.

'Grandma,' Jayden asked, breaking the silence, 'How did you find me?'

Grandma sighed. 'We used something called "The Spell of Shared Sight." Aria and I could see through your eyes. That's when we realised what the vampires were planning—they wanted to sacrifice you. We heard them whispering about it. We saw everything—your escape, their threats.' Grandma shook her head, as if shaking off the memory. 'It was... hard to watch.'

Aria shuddered at the thought, her heart tightening at the memory of seeing through Jayden's eyes. The panic, the fear—it had all felt too real, too close.

Jayden remained silent for a moment, his expression darkening. 'I didn't even know they were onto me until it was too late. I thought I was just following a lead about... the supernatural world. But once I was in, there was no backing out.'

Aria glanced over at him, her worry deepening. 'You didn't have to go through that alone, Jay.'

'I thought I could handle it,' Jayden admitted, his voice cracking slightly. 'I didn't want you dragged into it.'

Grandma, walking ahead of them, slowed her pace to match theirs. 'Well, you're both here now, safe. And that's what matters. But you should know, Jayden, the supernatural world isn't something you can just dabble in and walk away from. It has a way of pulling you back.'

Jayden nodded solemnly. 'I get that now. I really do.'

Aria squeezed his hand, her voice soft but firm. 'We'll deal with it together from now on. No more going off on your own.'

A faint smile touched his lips. 'I'll try not to.'

As they neared Grandma's shop, the comforting sight of the old, familiar building brought a sense of peace to them both. The chaos of the supernatural world faded away for a moment, replaced by the warmth of togetherness. It felt like, for the first time in a long while, they could breathe again.

As they approached the entrance to Grandma's shop, Jayden hesitated, his gaze dropping to the ground. 'There's something else I need to tell you both,' he began, his voice quiet but serious. Aria and Grandma both looked at him, sensing the weight of his words.

'A month ago, I found something,' Jayden continued, glancing up to meet their eyes. 'The Grimoire.'

'We know,' interrupted Aria. 'We tried a spell for making our memories clearer, by focusing on one object, and when I focused in the Grimoire, it showed me a distant memory of you flicking the pages of the Grimoire, though back then I thought that you were reading just a storybook,' Aria shrugged lightly.

'Well yeah, I found it around that time,' remarked Jayden. He hesitated for a moment, then sighed. 'The thing is... I didn't just stumble on the Grimoire by accident.'

Aria and Grandma turned their full attention to him, the air around them growing tense.

'It was hidden in my bedroom, beneath a loose board in the floor. I wasn't even looking for it... I was cleaning up some stuff when I accidentally knocked something over, and there it was, in this secret compartment.'

Grandma's face turned pale, her lips tightening in shock. 'Your bedroom? But the Grimoire was supposed to be safe in my care, locked away in my sanctuary,' she said, her voice shaky. 'How could it have ended up there?'

Aria furrowed her brow, then a terrible realisation hit her. 'Maria... it has to be Maria,' she whispered, anger creeping into her voice. 'She must've stolen it from you and hidden it in your bedroom.'

Jayden took a deep breath, his hands trembling slightly as he reached into his pocket and pulled out a folded piece of paper. 'There's something else,' he said quietly, almost as if speaking it aloud would make everything more real.

Aria and Grandma both turned toward him, their expressions already filled with concern. He hesitated for a moment before handing the paper to Aria. 'This was taped to the first page of the Grimoire when I found it.'

Aria unfolded the note, her brow furrowing as she read aloud: *'This Grimoire was given to you by Maria. Read it, and you'll understand what's coming.'*

Grandma gasped, her hands covering her mouth in shock. 'Maria... she left a message for you? That scab must have planned all of this! She wanted you to find it, to get drawn in.'

Jayden nodded, his face pale. 'I didn't know what to think when I found it. I should've told you, but... I thought I could handle it on my own. I didn't want to drag you both into this mess.'

Aria's hands shook slightly as she passed the note to Grandma. 'Maria... she wanted him to read the Grimoire. She was trying to lead him right to the vampires. This was a setup from the start.'

Grandma's face twisted with a mix of anger and sadness as she read the note, her voice filled with hurt. 'That traitor! She not only stole the Grimoire, but she deliberately put you in harm's way, Jayden. She knew the vampires would use it to lure you in.'

Jayden's voice was thick with regret. 'I thought I was doing the right thing by reading it, by trying to figure out what was happening. But Maria played me, just like she played all of us.'

Aria reached out and squeezed his hand. 'You couldn't have known, Jay. Maria manipulated you. None of this is your fault. But how do you even know about her?'

Jayden sighed; his voice heavy with frustration. 'I overheard the vampires talking. They kept praising Maria for how well she lured me in, saying she did the right thing by betraying the wizard coven and joining their side... stuff like that.'

Grandma's eyes flashed with fury. 'Maria is more dangerous than we thought. If she's willing to hand over the Grimoire to the vampires, who knows what else she's planning?'

'We'll secure the Grimoire, and then we'll deal with Maria. She may have tried to tear us apart, but we're stronger than she knows. This ends with us.' said Aria.

Grandma and Jayden nodded in agreement. 'Speaking of which, my darlings, would you mind staying here tonight? Your aunt and uncle wouldn't mind too, right?' Grandma asked.

'Of course they wouldn't mind, and so do we, but why?' Jayden asked, a bit puzzled.

'Well, this town believes you're dead, Jayden. I can't just go around telling them it wasn't an animal that attacked you but a vampire. People will think that I've gone mad. Well, they already think that I am—but imagine someone dead roaming around the streets. Not what you'd want to see, huh?' she explained with a wry smile, as Jayden and Aria smiled back. 'Aria, I'd suggest you take a day off school tomorrow, and we can figure out what to do next.'

'Got it, Grandma,' Aria nodded.

Jayden glanced around the small shack. 'But how are we all going to sleep here?' he asked, eyeing the cramped space.

'Oh, you've forgotten that I'm a witch, haven't you?' Elleira chuckled. She pulled her wand from her old-fashioned bag, which was slung on her shoulder, and flicked it with a look of focused concentration.

Slowly but surely, the tight space stretched and expanded, as if the room itself was breathing and growing larger. The ceiling rose higher, and the walls moved outward, revealing ornate patterns and decorations that hadn't been visible before.

Wooden beams arched overhead, and a warm glow filled the newly transformed hall. Where there had once been barely enough room to stand, there was now a grand, open space, complete with soft rugs, plush chairs, and two large beds in the centre.

'Whoa,' Jayden and Aria gasped in unison, wide-eyed at the transformation.

'I love magic.' Aria murmured, her voice filled with awe as she took in the massive, cosy room that had appeared before them.

'Nobody outside can see these, right?' Jayden asked, glancing nervously at the door as if expecting someone to walk in.

Grandma shook her head, a reassuring smile on her face. 'No one else can. This room is our little secret, just for us.'

With that comforting thought, Aria and Jayden settled onto their beds, which were remarkably soft and inviting. As they nestled into the plush pillows, Aria felt a wave of exhaustion wash over her.

The long battle they had fought—the heart-pounding chase, the fear of losing Jayden—felt distant now, yet it lingered in her mind as an unforgettable memory. She took a deep breath, letting the comfort of the moment envelope her.

'Goodnight, Aria, Grandma,' Jayden said dreamily, his voice barely above a whisper. 'Thank you for everything you've done for me. I wouldn't have made it without you.'

'Goodnight, dearies,' Grandma replied warmly, moving closer to tuck them in with a cosy blanket. She smoothed the fabric over them, her touch gentle and motherly. 'You both deserve all the rest you can get. Tomorrow is a new day.'

'Sweet dreams, Jay,' Aria whispered as she felt herself drifting into a world of beautiful dreams instead of the nightmares that had haunted her for so long. She pictured their adventures together, filled with laughter and light, and let that vision carry her into slumber.

The dream world was peaceful. Aria and Jayden wandered through sun-dappled fields, their laughter echoing in the air as they chased butterflies and marvelled at the blooming flowers. The warmth of the sun on her skin made everything feel so real, and for a brief, blissful moment, the weight of the night faded into nothingness.

They ventured deeper into a tranquil forest, where the trees seemed to hum with life. Every leaf, every branch, shimmered in colours that didn't exist in the waking world, like an enchanted paradise made just for them. They spoke of dreams and plans, of a future where danger was a distant memory.

As they walked together, the glow of the setting sun bathed everything in gold. Aria glanced over at her brother, who looked more carefree than he had in months. It was perfect—too perfect, perhaps. A nagging sensation began to tug at her mind, pulling her away from the warmth and beauty of the dream.

Jayden's laughter began to fade, replaced by an eerie silence. The golden hues of the forest dimmed, the vibrant colours draining from the world around them. Shadows began creeping in, their long, chalky white fingers stretching toward Aria, and her light-hearted dreams started to unravel.

She looked around frantically, her heart rate picking up as the once serene forest began to twist and distort. The trees, which moments ago had been alive with beauty, now loomed over her, dark and foreboding. A chill swept through the air, and she could no longer feel Jayden's presence beside her.

And then, in the blink of an eye, everything changed.

The happy memories, the vibrant colours, and the cheerful sights slowly gave way to the creeping horrors of the night.

Aria flinched as a cold mist curled around her feet, swirling in a familiar, unsettling way. The same landscape stretched before her—the vampire's clearing—the scene that had haunted her thoughts since that night.

In the dream, it felt even more vivid, as if she were reliving it.

Aria drifted toward the line of trees, though she had no idea why. Her steps felt heavy, as though she were sinking into the ground itself. Beneath the mist, something caught her eye—a faint glimmer.

She knelt, her fingers brushing against the cold earth, and there it was—a thin, sleek gold necklace half-buried in the dirt.

The delicate chain shimmered, and as her fingers carefully lifted it, a ring-shaped pendant swung loosely from the chain. Its surface was worn, scratched from years of wear or damage.

A strange sense of familiarity washed over her. She had seen this pendant before. It took her a moment, but then it struck her—a jolt of realisation that made her heart race.

This pendant... it had belonged to her mother. She had worn it every day, the same delicate chain that Aria had admired as a child.

Suddenly, the eerie scene vanished.

Aria jolted awake, gasping for breath, her chest rising and falling rapidly as she fought to steady herself.

Darkness still clung to the room, but her mind was aflame with the vivid remnants of the dream.

Every detail—the mist, the eerie clearing, and that necklace—burned with unsettling clarity.

Her body trembled, adrenaline surging through her veins as her wide eyes scanned the room, struggling to anchor herself back to reality.

Her heart pounded in her ears, drowning out the silence, as if her very soul refused to let go of the nightmare's grasp.

It was just a dream. It had to be.

But the chain—that necklace—its presence was too tangible, too real to dismiss. Her mother's necklace. The one that had vanished years ago without a trace.

How could it appear now, buried deep within the mist of her dream, as if waiting to be found?

About the Author

Aanya Diane is an enthusiastic thirteen-year-old author, with a big imagination and a deep passion for creativity. She loves reading fantasy novels, sketching her favourite characters, and spending time with her friends and family.

She has always been passionate about writing, using her creativity to bring unique stories to life. This is her first published book, and she is excited for her readers to enjoy the journey as much as she enjoyed writing it. She dreams of writing many more books and hopes her work encourages other young writers to explore their creativity and share their own stories.

www.ingramcontent.com/pod-product-compliance
Ingram Content Group UK Ltd.
Pitfield, Milton Keynes, MK11 3LW, UK
UKHW020246240426
12048UKWH00027B/1638